A DIFFERENCE OF OPINION

"There is a very simple answer to your frustration," Claredon murmured gently.

Victoria's brows arched. "You intend to magically disappear from my life?"

His eyes narrowed. "Have a child of your own."

A thick silence fell as she regarded him with disbelieving shock. Claredon couldn't deny he was rather shocked himself. He had given little thought to siring children. It had not seemed necessary until he discovered that perfect woman.

Oddly, however, he discovered himself swiftly becoming accustomed to the notion. He did not doubt Victoria would be an excellent mother, and he had every intention of being a devoted father. Why not begin a family?

Taking a sharp step backward, Victoria regarded him with an expression that warned him she was not nearly as accepting of the thought of creating a child as he was. "Do you never halt?" she asked. "You will say and do anything to get into my bed."

"You are not quite so irresistible as you believe, my dear. And I assure you that if I were that desperate to have you, I easily could have seduced you long ago."

"Not likely."

"It is a certainty." He closed the distance between them, reaching up to pluck the combs from her hair so the glossy tresses could tumble over her shoulders. "Shall I prove it here and now?"

Books by Debbie Raleigh

LORD CARLTON'S COURTSHIP

LORD MUMFORD'S MINX

A BRIDE FOR LORD CHALLMOND

A BRIDE FOR LORD WICKTON

A BRIDE FOR LORD BRASLEIGH

THE CHRISTMAS WISH

THE VALENTINE WISH

THE WEDDING WISH

A PROPER MARRIAGE

A CONVENIENT MARRIAGE

A SCANDALOUS MARRIAGE

Published by Zebra Books

A
SCANDALOUS
MARRIAGE

Debbie Raleigh

ZEBRA BOOKS
Kensington Publishing Corp.
http://www.kensingtonbooks.com

ZEBRA BOOKS are published by

Kensington Publishing Corp.
850 Third Avenue
New York, NY 10022

All Kensington titles, imprints and distributed lines are
available at special quantity discounts for bulk purchases for
sales promotion, premiums, fund-raising, educational or
institutional use.

Special book excerpts or customized printings can also be
created to fit specific needs. For details, write or phone the
office of the Kensington Special Sales Manager: Kensington
Publishing Corp., 850 Third Avenue, New York, NY 10022.
Attn. Special Sales Department. Phone: 1-800-221-2647.

Zebra and the Z logo Reg. U.S. Pat. & TM Off.

First Printing: March 2003
10 9 8 7 6 5 4 3 2 1

Printed in the United States of America

Prologue

It was only a dream.

But such an utterly delicious, sinfully wicked dream.

One moment Victoria Mallory was cursing the lumpy, dubiously clean mattress allotted to her at the posting inn just out side London, and the next she was slipping into an uneasy sleep that astonishingly included the sudden sensation of warm, male arms encircling her body and pulling her close to hard, naked muscles.

There was a brief flare of shock at the wanton pleasure shimmering through her, but as the dream also included a male voice whispering words of comfort and encouragement she slowly relaxed and allowed herself to loosen her stern restraint.

Why should she not, she sighed.

It surely was not so very sinful to dream of such delights? Soon enough she would be married to her beloved Thomas. He would hold her like this in his arms every evening.

Perhaps not with arms quite as large as those that enwrapped her in her dreams, she fuzzily conceded. Nor with fingers so cleverly experienced at untying the ribbons upon her nightrail. And unfortunately Thomas's one brief kiss had revealed wet, uncertain lips, not the strong, hungry lips currently devouring a path down the length of her arched neck.

Thomas's soft features fled as the hands became more impatient and the mouth lowered to the soft curve of her breast.

A new, rather startling heat seemed to be crystallizing in the very center of her being, a heat that poured through her body and made her bones feel as if they were melting.

It was a fierce, oddly fascinating sensation.

And at the same moment it sent a tingle of warning down her spine.

Although she was not one of those squeamish, high-strung maidens who feared the notion of the marriage bed, she could not deny a measure of unease. She had expected a sweet satisfaction when she at last gave herself to a man, a feeling of two souls melding to one, not this turbulent pleasure that set her heart racing and her body trembling with an unknown need.

The hands molded her ever closer and the seeking lips created havoc as they smoothly followed the line of her gaping bodice. She felt as if she were drowning in decadent delight, losing the control she so dearly treasured.

She faintly stiffened in wary confusion, but once again that dark, smoky voice was whispering in her ear.

It promised to cherish her, to worship her body and bring her pleasure beyond bearing.

Victoria discovered herself slowly relaxing as the tantalizing spell was woven about her. Then the voice suddenly groaned two husky words.

"Dearest Maria."

Victoria was roughly jerked from her dreams. With

an effort she wrenched open her eyes to discover a large, shadowed figure posed directly above her.

Dear lord, it was not a dream.

Some crazed madman had invaded her bed.

Shocked out of her wits, she opened her mouth and let forth a shrill scream of terror.

One

There were few things more ridiculous than a rotund vicar attired in a woefully snug coat, his few strands of gray hair standing upon end, attempting to tiptoe through the silent vicarage.

Vicar Humbly was not exactly frightened of his large, commanding housekeeper, he silently assured himself. She had been his devoted servant for near forty years. But he had no desire to wrangle with her so early in the morning.

He had already endured a fortnight of her grumblings at his determination to travel to Kent. She simply could not be made to understand his restless need to assure himself that Victoria was safely settled in her new life with Lord Claredon.

Humbly grimaced as he made his way down the stairs. In truth, he scarcely understood his odd behavior himself.

It had all begun weeks ago when he had received letters from Addy, Beatrice, and Victoria on the same morning. At the time it had seemed almost a sign from above.

How many nights had he devoted to worrying about their plight? Even though he had consented to officiate at each of their marriages over the past year, he had been plagued with doubts. Not one of the poor maidens had married for love, or even friendship.

His conscience had deeply troubled him, and when he received the letters he had known he must act. How could he happily retire to his small cottage when he was beset with worry over the happiness of the maidens?

And a good thing he had done so, he acknowledged with a faintly smug smile.

First he had traveled to London to help Addy in her marriage to Adam, then onto Derbyshire to give Beatrice and Gabriel a nudge. There was no doubt each had been in desperate straits when he arrived, and no doubt that he had managed to soothe troubled waters and ensure they could look into their hearts to discover the love waiting to be found.

Ah yes, he had been rather remarkable in his role as Cupid, he congratulated himself. Quite astonishing really.

Then his smile faltered.

Victoria was bound to be even more difficult than either Addy or Beatrice. Unlike the other two women, she had not thought to wed her husband. Indeed, she had been on the point of a secret elopement with a Mr. Stice when she had been trapped in a compromising position with Lord Claredon.

The marriage had been a hasty affair, as unwelcome as it was unexpected. And Humbly had stumbled through the vows with a prickling horror that the lovely bride might blacken the eye of her mocking bridegroom long before he could ever reach the "I do."

No, it would not be an easy task, he told himself with a faint sigh. Not easy at all.

"And just where do you think you are going?"

On the point of entering the foyer, Humbly reluctantly halted and turned to face the large, gray-haired servant who stood with her hands upon her hips. "Oh, Mrs. Stalwart," he murmured, feeling as guilty as a lad with his hand caught in a freshly baked pie.

Pie.

His large stomach grumbled, reminding him he had forsaken breakfast in the hopes of avoiding this encounter. A great sacrifice, indeed.

"I suppose you are determined to leave for Kent," she accused in tones dripping with disapproval.

"Yes, I did think that I might."

"'Tis unnatural, I tell you. Unnatural." The woman was swiftly off on her familiar tirade. "A gentleman of your advanced years should know better. First it was London and then Derbyshire, from where, I do not quibble to tell you, you came home appearing distinctly out of curl, and now it is Kent."

"I assure you that this shall be my last journey." He attempted to soothe the ruffled woman. "When I return I shall retire to my lovely cottage and never stir again."

The housekeeper gave an insulting snort. "So you keep promising."

"A promise I firmly intend to keep." The vicar was able to comfort her with all honesty.

Dissatisfied, the woman angled toward a new path. "What could possibly be so important in Kent?"

"I wish to ensure that Victoria, or I suppose I should say Lady Claredon, is well and happy in her marriage."

As expected, the older woman's countenance hardened. Although she possessed a kind heart, Mrs. Stalwart was not above indulging in the frivolous gossip that floated from London. It had been a deep disappointment when she learned Victoria had been embroiled in a sordid scandal. "A most ramshackle affair."

"Unfortunately, yes," the vicar murmured.

"I always knew that Lord Claredon would tumble into a bad end. He might be considered all that is handsome and charming, but he is a shameless rapscallion."

"Mrs. Stalwart."

"It is nothing but the truth," she plodded on, clearly laying the entire blame of the unfortunate incident upon the shoulders of the rakish Lord Claredon. "Do not try and pretend that you have not heard the whispers of his doings in London. It is said that he has a mistress for every night of the week."

Humbly attempted to appear shocked even as a renegade glimmer of amusement entered his sherry eyes. He had, of course, heard the endless gossip that swirled about Lord Claredon. He would have to be cloistered in the vicarage not to have. But possessing more than a hint of intelligence, he had dismissed most of the outrageous stories as envious chatter. No gentleman could be so virile, nor possess the vast amount of time required to seduce the hordes of women attributed to him.

"Really, Mrs. Stalwart, you know better than to listen to such rubbish."

"'Tis not rubbish," she determinedly argued, refusing to be swayed from her patent disapproval. "The man has gone to a good deal of effort to earn his reputation."

"Well, he has perhaps been a favorite among the ladies," Humbly reluctantly conceded.

"He is a reprehensible rake."

"No longer. He is now a married gentleman."

Mrs. Stalwart gave a sorrowful shake of her head, not at all reassured by the fact Lord Claredon had at least wed Victoria rather than leaving her a ruined woman.

"It near breaks my heart to think of my poor Victoria being taken in by his practiced charm," the housekeeper mourned, not fully aware of the tangled events that had led to Victoria and Lord Claredon being discovered together in the posting inn. "I had always thought her so sensible. Why, the way she took care of her younger sister after her parents' death and kept the household in order . . . I was never more shocked than when she tumbled into that nasty scandal."

Humbly's heart was struck by a sharp pang. Poor Victoria. After all she had sacrificed, she truly deserved happiness. A happiness he was far from certain could be found with Lord Claredon. Still, he was determined to do what was in his power to help her find a measure of contentment.

"Now, Mrs. Stalwart, we do not wish to stir old coals," he said firmly. "They are wed, and it is my fervent prayer that they have found a measure of peace."

The housekeeper gave a grudging nod of her head. "Aye. It is only that Victoria has always been a favorite of mine. She was so very brave during her parents' tragedy and then ensuring her sister was given everything a young girl could desire. It could not have been easy."

"No."

The older woman abruptly narrowed her gaze as she realized that she had been effectively distracted from her chastisement. "But I still do not understand the reason why you are traveling to Kent. Has Victoria requested your presence?"

Humbly cleared his throat. "Actually, I have decided to surprise her with a visit."

"Why?"

"To reassure myself that she is happy."

"Ha." Mrs. Stalwart wagged a finger in the direction of his overly innocent face. "You are going to meddle."

Humbly gave an offended sniff. "Certainly not."

"Do not think you can fool me. I have known you far too long."

He gave a rueful grimace. "I might nudge matters, if need be."

"Lord have mercy." The woman shook her head as if he were a hopeless trial upon her nerves. "I thought you wiser than to attempt to interfere between a husband and wife. There is nothing more foolish."

Humbly colored with defensive annoyance. "I will have you know that I have had no small measure of success at playing Cupid."

"Foolishness."

Knowing it was a futile argument, Humbly turned to gather his hat and gloves from the nearby table. "In any event, I hope to return by the end of the month."

Mrs. Stalwart crossed her arms over her considerable bosom. "And those books you have promised to pack before the new vicar arrives?"

He flashed his particularly sweet smile. "They will no doubt be awaiting me when I return."

"Foolishness," the housekeeper muttered.

Two

Victoria was casually sketching the bloom of a rose in the conservatory when the young maid rushed in to inform her that a Mr. Humbly had come to call.

Dropping her pad and charcoal onto the bench she surged to her feet in startled disbelief. It had been over five months since she had last set eyes upon the sweet, endearingly absentminded vicar—not since the day he had irrevocably tied her to the gentleman who had ruined her life.

A flare of panic raced through her as she regarded the maid with a disbelieving gaze. "Are you certain he said Humbly?" she absurdly demanded.

"Yes, my lady. Shall I tell him you are not receiving visitors?"

"No." Victoria sucked in a steadying breath. "Please show him into the front salon and inform him that I shall join him in a moment."

"At once."

With a curtsy, the servant hurried away, and Victoria left the comforting privacy of the conservatory.

She supposed that deep within her she was not entirely shocked by the sudden arrival of Vicar Humbly. He had not bothered to hide his distress when she had requested that he call the banns, nor when he had stood at the altar and proclaimed her wife to

Lord Claredon. More than once he had sought to lure her aside and discuss her upcoming life with her husband. But Victoria had firmly avoided his kindly interference.

As much as she might love the gentle vicar, there was nothing he could say or do to make her lot more bearable—not unless he could undo that ghastly night that had forever altered her placid existence.

A small shiver shook her body as the memory of the moment she had opened her eyes to discover Lord Claredon in bed with her rose reluctantly to mind.

What horrid fate had occurred to bring the two of them together? If only Thomas had not become confused and gone to the wrong posting inn. If only she had not chosen to hide her identity by using the name of her distant cousin, Lady Westfield. If only Lord Claredon had not arrived and promptly presumed Lady Westfield would be anxious to enjoy a bit of seduction.

If only . . .

Squaring her shoulders, Victoria shifted her route and made her way toward the back of the house, where her husband was no doubt busy with the endless paperwork involved in running his estate.

She could not change the "if onlys," but she could hopefully avoid the unwelcome pity that Mr. Humbly was bound to offer. Enduring the scandal of being found in the bed of England's most notorious rogue was bad enough. She would not add fodder to the gossips by allowing others to know she was just as miserable as all had predicted when she became Lady Claredon.

Her hopes for the future might lie in tatters, but she did have her pride. For whatever that was worth.

Victoria halted before the closed door of the study, briefly experiencing a sense of unease.

It was not that she feared her husband, she acknowledged. Claredon was certainly never violent, nor did he possess a harsh tongue. But she had come to dread the taunting mockery that set her nerves upon edge and the restless brooding in his deep blue eyes. It was rather like living with a sleek tiger that pretended to be tamed, but who smoldered with a restrained power that might be unsheathed at any moment.

With an impatient shake of her head, Victoria thrust aside her absurd fancies. She had made a determined decision during the long journey to Kent: She would not allow herself to be intimidated by her sophisticated, worldly husband. Over the years, she had learned to be a strong, independent woman. She would use her skills to forge a place as Lady Claredon.

Not bothering to knock, she pushed open the door and stepped into the austere, distinctly masculine room dominated by a heavy Sheridan desk. The magnificent plasterwork on the ceiling was nicely revealed by the large windows that overlooked the terraced garden, and the walls were lined with heavy bookcases that held the large ledgers tracing the history of the estate for the past century.

It was a room that smelled of leather and purely masculine pursuits, more than a touch forbidding to a mere woman.

Swallowing heavily, she stepped forward at the same moment Claredon rose to his feet. Victoria stumbled to a nervous halt. Even after five months of marriage, she was still caught off guard by his sheer physical beauty. Gads, it was little wonder that he had been so sought after by women eager to join his collection of mistresses.

Standing well over six feet, he possessed a form that was a tailor's dream. His shoulders were broad, his waist lean, and his long legs crafted to wear the form-fitting buff breeches. His raven dark hair was brushed casually toward a countenance that had been masterfully chiseled, and his deep blue eyes were thickly fringed. As if the angels had not been satisfied with his breathtaking perfection, they had added a pair of roguish dimples that could melt the hardest of hearts.

All except her own, she sternly reminded herself. She was thoroughly impervious to the irresistible Lord Claredon.

Thoroughly.

As if able to read her defiant thoughts, Claredon allowed his gaze to roam slowly over her simple buttercup gown that nicely complimented her dark titian curls and pure green eyes.

"Good God," he drawled in that hateful voice. "Has the sun toppled to the ground? Or perhaps the tenants have revolted?"

Her brows snapped together at his annoying tone. "I beg your pardon?"

He moved to lean negligently against the corner of the desk. "Well, after five months of marriage, this is the first occasion that you have deliberately sought me out. I presume only a disaster of scandalous proportions could have induced you."

She refused to rise to the bait as her chin tilted upward. "Not precisely a disaster. Vicar Humbly has arrived."

"Humbly?" It took a moment before he smiled

with wry comprehension. "Ah, the cheerful, rather dim-witted fool who wed us."

"He is not a fool," she retorted in clipped tones.

He offered a mocking bow of his head. "No, you are correct, my dear, as always. I sensed more beneath his vague distraction than he cared to reveal."

She resisted the urge to put a crook in that perfect masculine nose. Gads, but he annoyed her. And she did not doubt for a moment that it was entirely on purpose.

"He can be quite perceptive when he chooses," she forced herself to say in even tones. "And he is not above interfering in matters that do not necessarily concern him."

"A meddler?"

"Only in the most subtle manner. In truth you rarely realize he has even meddled until he has steered you in the direction he has desired."

The blue eyes slowly narrowed. "So what is he doing in Kent?"

"I do not know."

"Would it not be a simple matter to ask him?"

She gave a restless shrug. "I will."

"But there is something troubling you?"

Now that it came to the moment, Victoria discovered herself faltering. The impulse to salvage her pride had been much simpler when not confronting her unpredictable husband. "I would prefer that he not realize . . ."

"Yes?" he prompted.

She squared her shoulders. "That our marriage is a fraud."

"A fraud?" His raven brows lifted as he flicked a glance over her stiff form. "Dear heavens. Do you know, I possess a distinct memory of standing before the vicar as we said our vows. How very odd. Of course, the fact that our marriage is a fraud would explain the strange lack of a bride in my bed."

Her hard-won composure shattered at his deliberate barb at her refusal to perform her wifely duty. "Perhaps a lack of a bride in your bed, but not a lack of a woman," she charged before she could halt the words.

He stilled as her unruly accusation hung heavy in the air. "Are you asking if I seek my husbandly comforts elsewhere?"

"Not at all," she muttered, cursing her wayward tongue. The last thing she desired was for him to know how the thought of him with other women gnawed deep within her. She far preferred him to believe she was utterly indifferent. "What do I care?"

His smile remained, but the lean features abruptly hardened. "Yes, indeed. What do you care?"

"We are straying from the subject."

"Of course," he mocked. "We would not wish to discuss the fact I possess an unwilling wife."

Her hands clenched at her side. Oh, yes. One day soon she would bloody that nose. "Is that all you can ever think of, Claredon?" she charged.

"Do you never think of it, my dear?" he smoothly countered.

She gave a shake of her head as she stepped back toward the door. "I knew this would be a waste of my time."

"Hold." He abruptly straightened. "What is it that you wanted?"

She wavered, longing to flee from his aggravating presence and yet still hopeful she could avoid further gossip. At last her lingering horror of the speculative glances and whispered comments halted her retreat.

She forced herself to meet his gaze squarely. "I hoped that we could keep our ridiculous squabbles in private. I have no desire to worry Vicar Humbly or to stir yet more unnecessary gossip. I have endured enough scandal."

He appeared amused by her halting words. "You believe we can convince the good vicar we are happily wed?"

"I would hope we could at least be civil."

"My dear, I am always civil," he drawled.

It took an absurd effort not to stamp her foot in frustration. "No, you are always deliberately provoking," she gritted. "I realize that you take great delight in riling my temper, but I would appreciate it if you would resist the temptation."

"You do your own share of provoking, Victoria." His gaze deliberately lowered to the low cut of her neckline. "And far more cruelly than I."

Her hands instinctively lifted to cover the skin that tingled from the heat of his gaze. It infuriated her that despite the fact that this gentleman had ruined her life, despite the fact that he was an insatiable rake, her body still reacted to his mere presence.

No, not just reacted, she brutally admitted. Shivered, quivered, and downright lusted. It was odiously unfair. "I do not know why I bother," she muttered, turning on her heel to storm from the room.

The man was impossible, she told herself as she made her way toward the front salon. Granted, he had been no more pleased than she to be forced into marriage, she reluctantly conceded. And he had at least not left her to face the scandal on her own.

But there was no excuse for his determined delight in tormenting her. They could go along quite well if only he would follow her lead and maintain a cool civility. To be always baiting her and stirring her ready temper ensured their life together was in constant turmoil.

Forcing herself to halt before the parlor door, Victoria took in a calming breath and smoothed her hands down her muslin skirt. She had been a fool to approach Claredon. It would be up to her to distract Humbly from the truth of her marriage.

Hoping she did not appear as flushed and flustered as she felt, Victoria forced herself to step into the room. Although not large, it was prettily painted in a soft lavender, with Parisian paper panels adding a nice hint of elegance. The oak furnishings were covered with an ivory silk that was echoed in the draperies.

At her entrance, the rotund gentleman attired in black rose to his feet.

A portion of her nervous unease faded as he offered her a sweet smile. Barely aware she was moving, she crossed the carpet to clasp his hands. "Mr. Humbly, how delightful you have called," she said, not entirely lying. The vicar carried with him an air of unshakable peace that was very soothing to her taut nerves.

"My dear Victoria." He stepped back to eye her in obvious approval. "How wonderful you look. Marriage must agree with you."

She swallowed a hysterical urge to laugh. Marriage agree with her? More likely the plague would agree with her. "Yes," she managed to choke out before she hurriedly changed the subject. "Tell me, what brings you to Kent?"

The sherry eyes softened. "You, of course, my dear."

She attempted to appear surprised. "Me?"

"I have been concerned."

"That is very kind," she assured him, "but there was no need."

His brows lifted. "Was there not? Although I cannot claim an expertise in marriage, I realize that it cannot have been easy to wed a near stranger under such circumstances."

"It has been an adjustment," she conceded, knowing that the vicar was far too wise to be easily fooled.

"I just wished to assure myself that you are happy."

Victoria abruptly moved to settle upon an ivory sofa. "Will you not have a seat?"

"Thank you." He lowered his bulk upon a trellis-backed chair, his steady gaze never wavering from her guarded countenance. He could be as tenacious as a bill collector when he desired. "Now, my dear, tell me how you go on."

She folded her hands in her lap and sent up a prayer of forgiveness for the lies she was about to utter. Surely a kindly God would understand her distaste for further gossip. "Very well, I thank you. I have been quite busy restoring the estate. It has been a number of years since it was last occupied."

He dutifully glanced about the room, patiently allowing himself to be distracted. "You are to be congratulated. It is so refreshing to enter a home that is not so stiffly formal you fear to move in case you tumble a priceless heirloom to the floor."

Victoria smiled. She had been pleasantly surprised by the comfortable estate. Claredon's parents, the Earl and Countess of Moreland, lived in a stiff mausoleum that had made her dread what to expect in Kent. This plain brick home, with two sweeping wings and a lovely conservatory, was far more to her taste.

"Thank you. This estate is far too small for any pretense of formality."

"Just the perfect size."

"Yes, I think so."

His gaze returned to her wary eyes. "And how is Lord Claredon?"

"I fear he is busy with the tenants and overseeing the coming harvest," she replied, hoping Claredon possessed the goodness to stay far away from their guest. If he would not be of help, then at least he could avoid interfering with her own attempts to soothe Mr. Humbly's doubts. "He is quite dedicated to introducing the latest farming techniques."

"An admirable sentiment," the vicar swiftly approved. "I believe England's greatness depends upon staying well ahead of other countries."

"Lord Claredon is certainly doing his part," she was able to retort with all honesty.

"I do hope he will not protest to an uninvited interloper?"

"Not at all. He will be delighted to have a guest."

"And you?"

Victoria managed to keep her smile intact. "I am very pleased you have come, although it was not at all necessary for you to travel such a distance. Did you not receive my letter?"

"I did, indeed," he retorted with a rather mysterious expression. "Which is precisely why I have come."

She eyed him in surprise. "But I assured you that all was well."

"With a bit too much vehemence, I fear."

Victoria felt her cheeks warm in embarrassment. Gads, she should have taken more care. She knew how perceptive he could be beneath his vague air. "That is absurd," she attempted to bluff.

"Is it?"

"Of course. As I said, I have settled into marriage quite comfortably."

"And you are happy?" he charged.

She shifted upon the cushions. "How could I not be? I have managed to wed the most sought after gentleman in all of England."

"Being the most sought after bachelor does not ensure a comfortable husband," he retorted in dry tones. "Nor a blissful marriage."

She shivered. No, there was nothing comfortable about Claredon. Nor had marriage been particularly blissful. More like being tossed onto a battlefield.

Hopelessly searching for some means to divert the all too shrewd vicar, Victoria was relieved when the door to the parlor was pushed open. The relief was short-lived, however, as the lean form of Claredon stepped into the room.

She rose to her feet, along with Humbly, already feeling her nerves tangling in apprehension. Why the devil had he intruded when she had specifically told him she wished to avoid their fiery confrontations, she silently seethed. Did he intend to deliberately embarrass her just out of spite?

Moving with the peculiar grace of a predator, he crossed to offer a bow to Humbly. Then, before she could guess his intention, he shifted to stand far too close to her stiff form. She flashed him a wary glance as with a wicked smile he boldly slid an arm about her shoulders. "My dearest, forgive me for being delayed. Dunford insisted I inspect the quarterly reports."

His sweet breath stirred the curls upon her cheek, making Victoria shiver with awareness. He was too close. And she did not trust the dangerous fire that smoldered in those deep blue eyes. What the devil was he doing?

"I . . . Mr. Humbly has come to visit," she at last managed to mumble.

"A most welcome guest."

"Thank you," Humbly retorted, regarding the gentleman's intimate hold upon Victoria with open speculation.

"Is this your first visit to Kent?"

"Yes, it is."

"Ah, we shall have to ensure you see some of the local sights." Claredon turned his head to meet her narrowed gaze. "What do you think, my turtle dove? Perhaps we should drive to Canterbury—or, if the good vicar prefers, we could make a visit to Chilham Castle and the Church of St. Mary. I am sure he will be impressed by its fifteenth-century tower."

With an effort, she attempted to thrust aside the sizzling awareness that threatened to buckle her knees. It was obvious that Claredon had reconsidered her request and had decided to enter her charade. She should, no doubt, be grateful for his unexpected change of heart. Unfortunately, she had not entirely considered her renegade reaction to his presence when she had so impulsively sought his help.

"I am sure Mr. Humbly would find any of them fascinating," she said in uneven tones.

His fingers aimlessly moved to stroke the bare skin of her shoulder. Victoria caught her breath as a scorching heat raced through her blood at his casual caress.

"And we must think of entertaining," he murmured, turning his attention to the silent vicar. "I fear that Victoria and I have been sadly reclusive since coming to Longmeade. We have preferred to maintain our privacy, as I am certain you will understand."

"Oh, yes." Humbly gave a faint cough. "Yes, indeed."

"Now, however, we must think of inviting a few of the neighbors." Audaciously he lowered his head to brush his lips over the sensitive skin of her temple. "I suppose it does not do to keep my beautiful bride to myself, no matter how much I might desire to do so."

"Oh, please, do not bother on my account," Humbly protested, thankfully not noticing how Victoria's knees threatened to give way.

"Nonsense, it is no bother," she said, futilely attempting to put a measure of space between herself and the hard male body. "We have neglected our neighbors quite shamelessly."

Claredon gave a low chuckle as his damnable fingers moved to trace the line of her throat.

"Ah, but what a delicious reason we have had for neglecting them. Others are quite understanding of those upon their honeymoon. Do you not agree, Mr. Humbly?"

"Oh, certainly. Most understandable."

"Especially when one is fortunate enough to have acquired such a beautiful bride," Claredon drawled.

Victoria briefly considered stomping upon her husband's foot. Gads, but he was annoying. She had requested that he be polite, not asked him to seduce her in front of their guest.

"Claredon, I do not believe Mr. Humbly is interested in hearing of our honeymoon," she gritted in overly sweet tones.

"No, no. I am delighted to know that you have both settled into marriage so well," Humbly assured her, although a question of doubt remained in his sherry eyes.

"Ah, we have more than settled, have we not, my sweetness?" Claredon murmured. "We are wallowing in marital bliss."

Victoria knew what she would like to see Claredon wallowing in. A midden heap came to mind. "I . . . yes."

Humbly smiled. "That is lovely."

Angry, and not a little anxious to put an end to Claredon's seductively distracting touch, Victoria determinedly stepped away from his large form. "I should ensure Mrs. Troy has a room prepared for our guest."

"No, you remain with the good vicar," her husband swiftly countered. "I shall speak with Mrs. Troy. Then I fear I must return to the fields. I shall be back in time for dinner."

A cowardly relief ran through her. "Very well."

Easily reading her thoughts, Claredon gave a low chuckle before swiftly moving forward to claim a brief, shattering kiss. He pulled back, a hint of satisfaction curving his lips at her uncontrollable shudder of excitement. "Do not miss me too much while I am gone," he murmured.

Effectively robbed of speech, Victoria watched in silence as Claredon nodded toward the vicar, then turned to leave the room.

It was the first kiss they had shared since that fateful night that had altered both of their lives.

Victoria had made it fiercely clear she did not desire his kisses. What else could she do? She had known all along that such intimacies would only lead to danger. Being an innocent did not mean she was completely naive. And as difficult as it might be to admit, she had known since her wedding that she was no more immune to Claredon's rakish charm than any other nitwitted maiden.

She had no desire to be one more conquest. The mere thought was unbearable.

Belatedly gathering her shaken composure, Victoria turned to meet Mr. Humbly's speculative gaze.

"Well, it appears that my worries have been for naught," he murmured.

Victoria forced a smile to her stiff lips. It was precisely what she had desired. A shiver shook her body. So why did she feel as if she had just loosened a wild tiger from its cage?

"Yes."

Three

As he indicated, Claredon spent the day in the fields with his tenants. It was a task he relished.

Unlike many noblemen, he did not consider his land and workers as necessary burdens to be endured to keep him in luxury. He truly enjoyed farming.

He liked the smell of rich earth early in the morning, watching the seedlings grow to healthy crops, and rejoicing when the harvest was bountiful. He enjoyed experimenting with new techniques and radical notions that were shunned by the more traditional landowners. He even enjoyed getting his hands dirty and calloused as he worked beside his tenants.

Today, however, he could not deny that his smile was a bit wider and his step a bit lighter. The memory of Victoria's telling shudder as he had kissed her lingered with a sweet vengeance.

He had known that beneath her fiery disdain was a passion that matched his own. Only her ridiculous pride forced her to deny them the pleasure that could easily be theirs. Perhaps with Humbly's unexpected but timely arrival, he would at last possess the opportunity to prove it to her.

If nothing else, it would at least force her to spend more time in his company, he acknowledged as he made his way back to the manor house. Since coming to Longmeade, she had treated him as little better than a leper. He had been left in no doubt that she had held him fully responsible for the disaster that had led to their hasty marriage.

She would not accept she was at least partially to blame for being alone in a posting inn and for posing as her elegant cousin, who had been ruthlessly pursuing him for the past six months. Certainly she never appeared to consider the notion he was as much a victim of the ghastly mix-up as herself. He had not desired to wed—not, at least, until he had discovered the perfect maiden.

As the youngest and only son with seven older sisters, he had been cosseted and spoiled his entire life. He had also developed a fine appreciation for the fairer sex.

What could be better than their tantalizing scent, their tinkling laughter and soft touch? He fully enjoyed filling his life with women, all sorts of women, from beautiful to exotic to mysterious.

But having been raised by a notorious rake, he had realized his love for women carried a heavy cost. Although the Earl of Moreland was deeply devoted to his family, Claredon had been painfully aware of his mother's distress when his father would seek the company of yet another doxy. Lady Moreland loved her husband too deeply not to feel betrayed by his casual affairs and the unmistakable proof of his byblows being flaunted throughout the countryside.

So while Claredon was quite willing to indulge his sensuous nature, he had made an unshakable promise he would remain faithful once he was wed. His own wife would never endure the pain of betrayal, nor his children harbor an inner disappointment in his lack of respect for their mother. The only answer was to find the one utterly unblemished maiden who could bewitch his heart, challenge his mind, and ensure his devotion never wavered.

A difficult task, he had readily acknowledged, but it was no punishment to search through England for this paragon. Not when the search was readily spiced with the enjoyment of willing women who did not have marriage upon their mind.

Now his well-schemed plans lay in ruins.

Instead of his fantasy maiden, he was wed to a sharp-tongued, ill-tempered shrew who was determined to make his life a misery. Even worse, while he had kept to his vow of faithfulness, Victoria refused to allow him the pleasure of his marital bed. There had been a few times over the past days when he wondered why he bothered. Victoria did not love him. She did not even particularly like him. She could not be hurt if he decided to take a mistress.

And heaven above knew that short of a biblical miracle, there was no hope for children to be disappointed in his behavior. But as swiftly as the treacherous thoughts would enter his mind, he thrust them aside. The brutal truth was that he did not desire another woman.

Even though he had barely been allowed to taste the tempting sweetness of his wife's passion, it had been enough to stir to life an aching need. The satin softness of her skin, the warm scent of lilacs, and the ready heat of her lips lingered in his mind with a maddening tenacity. He could not close his eyes at night without dreaming of holding her in his arms. To simply watch her cross a room was enough to grip him with a stark hunger.

The knowledge was as disturbing as it was unexpected.

Never before had he been plagued by such frustrated desire. He did not seduce innocents or those women who preferred to play coy games of seduction. He was accustomed to women who readily pursued him, women who were anxious to fulfill their mutual passions. Not one of those women had ever made him pace the floor during the long night or battle the constant need to seek out her company simply for the pleasure of hearing her voice.

It was little wonder he took such delight in baiting her. He would not be the only one in torment.

With a shake of his head at his decidedly childish thoughts, Claredon entered the house and made his way to his chambers.

As always, his valet was awaiting his return. With swift efficiency, Claredon discovered himself bathed and properly attired in a dark blue coat and ivory waistcoat.

Sending the servant from the room, he tied his cravat into a precise knot and was debating between the ruby or diamond stickpins when there was a sharp rap upon his door. With a faint frown, he turned from the dressing table. "Enter."

There was a brief pause before the door was at last pushed open. Astonishingly, his wife stepped into his room.

Against his will, his heart trembled at her presence.

It was not just her beauty—although there was no denying she was lovely, with those thick titian curls and eyes the color of finest emeralds. It was more the power of her spirit and elegant strength of her tall form.

This was a woman who would face the world with

her chin held high, regardless of the adversity she might face. And heaven help anyone foolish enough to try and stand in her way.

She colored faintly as his gaze compulsively lowered to appreciate the moss green silk gown that gave such a tempting hint of the womanly curves beneath. Her chin abruptly jutted in the air as she regarded him as if he had just crawled from beneath a moldy rock. "I must speak with you," she stated in sharp tones.

Inwardly bristling at her odious habit of treating him as a particularly loathsome creature, Claredon leaned against the dressing table and offered her a taunting smile. "Well, well, my dear, you have sought me out for the second time in one day. I begin to feel quite irresistibly attractive."

Her aquiline nose flared. "You know quite well why I am here."

"To tell the truth, I haven't the least notion," he drawled, his smile widening. "Dare I hope it is with the intention of seducing me?"

"Certainly not."

"A pity." He lazily surveyed the enticing plunge of her neckline. "I have been thinking all day how extraordinarily soft your skin felt beneath my fingers. As soft as I remember from our night together."

She glared at him, but she could not disguise the revealing flutter of her pulse at the base of her neck.

Claredon barely resisted the maddening urge to press his lips to that pulse.

"Would you please halt your baiting of me?"

"I am not baiting you. I am merely revealing my thoughts during the long afternoon. Does it disturb you to know that I desire my wife?"

Her color deepened. "It disturbs me to know you desire every woman who crosses your path."

"Oh, not every woman," he denied, not at all displeased by the sharp edge in her tone. Could it be she was just a tad jealous of these mythical other women? "And none with the intensity that I desire you."

"I never wished you to desire me."

His lips twisted, not above a bit of jealousy himself. It was never far from his mind that his wife had been on the point of eloping with a spineless, witless fool when they had encountered one another. "No, of course not. You prefer passionless gentlemen who are more in need of a mother than a wife."

Her eyes widened. "That is a horrid thing to say."

"It is nothing more than the truth," he retorted without apology. "You treated poor Mr. Stice more as a sickly child than a potential lover."

"What do you know of how I treated Thomas?"

Claredon abruptly paused. What did he know? Certainly the limited London Society ensured that they were occasionally attending the same function, and she was striking enough to have demanded more than a glance or two. Still, he had not realized until this moment just how often his gaze must have strayed in her direction.

Uncomfortable with the realization, he gave a restless shrug. "He trailed behind you like a cowering pup."

"You . . ." Her hands clenched at her side as if battling the urge to blacken his eye. "You of all people have no right to judge Thomas. At least he could make a binding commitment to another, something you are incapable of."

He lifted his dark brows. "Have you gone mad? I have made the most irrevocable commitment possible. Or have you forgotten that I was the one to stand before the altar beside you, not your precious Thomas?"

Her face abruptly paled. "Dear God, how could I forget?"

A sharp annoyance raced through him. How many maidens would have given anything to wed him? How many would be dancing a jig at such good fortune? Instead, Victoria still mourned the pathetic wretch who could not even travel to the proper posting inn.

"It is time to forget him, Victoria. Whatever evil fate brought us together in that posting inn has ensured that we are bound together for eternity."

"Forgive me, but, unlike you, I do not easily forget those I care about."

He slowly straightened. He would endure many things, but no one could expect him to ignore being considered an inferior specimen to the likes of Mr. Thomas Stice. She was his wife. She owned him her loyalty, if nothing else. "Take care, Victoria. I have endured enough of your insults."

She briefly faltered at the lethal edge in his tone, then predictably she squared her shoulders in defiance. "Do you deny that you were an incurable rake?"

"I admit that I have always possessed a full appreciation for women."

Her features hardened with distaste. "An appreciation that would fade as swiftly as it began. I will not be one more of a very large collection."

"I wonder why it is you continue to dredge up my less than pure past with such monotonous regularity." He narrowed his eyes. "Are you afraid you might forget that I am a rake and a libertine?"

"Never."

"That is a considerable length of time, my precious." Claredon moved deliberately forward, not halting until the warm scent of lilacs surrounded him. "Especially when you have requested that I play the role of doting husband."

The delicious pulse began to flutter again. "That is precisely what I wished to discuss with you."

"Am I not being attentive enough?" he murmured, lifting his hand to toy absently with a titian curl that lay upon her cheek. "Forgive me, but I had promised my steward I would ensure the wagon was repaired, as well as overseeing the work on the bridge. I assure you I can offer my undivided attention from this evening onward. Indeed, I am determined to be at your side night and day." He heard her breath catch, sending a feather of excitement curling through his stomach.

"You are being absurd," she protested.

"Am I? I thought you were the one who was desperate to convince Vicar Humbly we are madly in love."

Her tongue peeked out to wet her dry lips, and his excitement became more pronounced. And considerably more urgent. Blast! What he wouldn't give to press her against the door and explore her honeyed temptation.

"I requested that you be civil, not make a cake of yourself."

"I apologize." His hand restlessly moved to stroke the line of her cheek. He considered daring his luck to steal a kiss, only to conclude he was rather fond of his nose the way it was. "Having seven sisters married, I presumed that all bridegrooms behaved like mooncalves. Certainly my brothers-in-law regularly make perfect twits of themselves."

"Humbly is well aware that ours was not a normal courtship. It will be enough merely to be polite to one another."

"I disagree."

"I beg your pardon?"

"Humbly was obviously concerned enough to travel a considerable distance to visit you. I do not believe he will be reassured by cool civility between us."

She paused as if grudgingly considering his logic. Very grudgingly, he wryly conceded as her lips thinned in frustration.

"Perhaps there should be a certain amount of warmth."

He gave a click of his tongue, his fingers teasing her tight lips. "A considerable amount of warmth, if you do not wish Humbly to return to Surrey with word that he made a dreadful mistake in officiating our wedding. Gentlemen such as the vicar are incurably romantic by nature. Regardless of our reasons for a hasty marriage, he will desire to see us giddy with happiness."

She took a sharp step backward, only to come up against the door. "You have made your point, Claredon. That does not, however, give you leave to . . ."

"Yes?" he prompted with a wicked smile.

"Maul me."

He gave a sharp bark of laughter. "I hardly consider a few light caresses and a brief kiss as mauling you."

Her emerald eyes flashed at his taunting words. "You do not fool me. This is merely an opportunity to punish me for not allowing you into my bed."

"Now you are the one being absurd, Victoria."

"Really?"

"I have no desire to punish you." He offered her the arrogant smile he knew set her teeth on edge. "Not when I know with all certainty that it is only a matter of time before you welcome me to your bed. It is as inevitable as the sun rising tomorrow."

She sucked in an audible breath. "You must be out of your senses."

His gaze deliberately lowered to the lush promise of her lips. "You have not forgotten how you shivered beneath my touch any more than I have. I had barely kissed you when you were pleading for more."

She shivered at the undeniable truth in his words. "I was asleep," she fiercely retorted.

"And dreaming of Mr. Stice?"

"I . . . yes."

"Liar," he mocked. "Had he been in your thoughts, you never would have melted with such obvious delight."

"How dare you?"

"I dare because I know quite well that had you responded to the pudding-faced fool with such trembling eagerness, you would not be the innocent maiden you are today."

She flushed, making Claredon wonder if it were from outrage or guilt. "You are horrid."

He gave a nonchalant shrug. "Horrid or not, you desire me. And eventually that desire will overcome your ridiculous pride."

She gave a rather desperate shake of her head. "When cows learn to waltz."

Claredon chuckled, cupping her chin in a firm grasp. "I hear the orchestra tuning up."

If Victoria had scoured England from one end to another, she could not have discovered a more arrogant, more annoying, more . . . obnoxious gentleman to wed than Lord Claredon.

Nearly four hours after fleeing from her husband's chambers, she was still battling her raw nerves.

It was difficult enough to struggle with her renegade awareness of Claredon. Now, with the knowledge he was fully conscious of that awareness, she longed to sink beneath the floorboards.

Even worse was the sudden realization that far from being reconciled to her declaration she would never truly be his wife, he had been toying with her like a cat with a hopeless mouse, merely biding his time until her pride faltered and she begged to have him in her bed.

Victoria shuddered, wishing she could be certain such a humiliating fate was not possible. Unfortunately, she was far too honest with herself to turn a blind eye to the danger. At least she had been granted a brief reprieve, she acknowledged with a faint sigh.

After dinner, Claredon had been cornered by his steward, who had demanded a few moments of his time. Victoria had been quite happy to lead Vicar Humbly to the salon without the disturbing presence of her husband.

Glancing across the room to where the vicar sipped his brandy with obvious appreciation, she forced her futile broodings from her mind. Such troubles would have to be put aside for now. It was more important to lay the vicar's concerns to rest.

"I do hope that you have settled in comfortably, Mr. Humbly," she said in a deliberately light tone.

"Yes, indeed. And may I say you have an artist in the kitchen? Her salmon was simply divine."

"Mrs. Boland is very accomplished. I believe you will also be pleased with her pastries."

The vicar patted his stomach, a twinkle in his sherry eyes. "Ah, you have not forgotten my love for pastries."

"Of course not. And I have ensured that there will be plenty of cakes and tarts to choose from."

He heaved a pleased sigh. "I was quite certain that I would enjoy visiting your lovely estate. Now there can be no doubt."

A portion of Victoria's tension eased at the dear gentleman's gentle humor. "Well, I do hope we can offer you more in the way of entertainment than a few trifling pastries."

"My dear, you do not know what you are saying," he retorted. "You will learn that when a gentleman reaches my advanced years, attending to the needs of his stomach is quite entertainment enough."

"Nonsense," she protested with a laugh. "You have always been the most inexhaustible gentleman I have ever known. I recall you sitting at the bedside of an ill villager throughout the night and yet spending the entire day visiting the local cottages and even enduring a tedious dinner with that wretched Squire Irwin without so much as a yawn."

Humbly gave a sad shake of his head. "Those days are past, my dear. Indeed, I shall soon be retiring to my small cottage."

Victoria widened her eyes in shock. "Retiring? You cannot mean to do so."

"Yes, and I assure you that I quite look forward to my lazy days of doing nothing more than tending to my roses."

Victoria found it nearly impossible to imagine the vicarage without Mr. Humbly. "But whatever will the neighborhood do without you?"

He waved a pudgy hand, but there was a hint of gratitude upon his round countenance.

"They will survive quite nicely, I am certain. The new vicar is quite young and anxious to set the church in order."

Victoria shook her head, knowing no one could

ever replace this compassionate and generous man. "It will not be the same."

"All will be well," he said firmly. "It is time."

Before Victoria could retort, the door was abruptly thrust open and Claredon entered the room. Waving a hand toward the vicar, who was struggling to rise, he moved deliberately across the carpet to settle on the sofa, far too close to Victoria's suddenly stiff body.

"Forgive me for taking so long," he murmured, smoothly laying his arm along the back of the sofa and allowing his fingers to lightly brush her shoulder. "My steward possesses a tedious belief that I desire to be informed of the most insignificant details connected to the estate."

"I should think he is not far off in his belief," the vicar murmured shrewdly.

Claredon chuckled. "Perhaps not. I hope Victoria has kept you well entertained."

"But of course."

Cursing her foolishness in not having chosen one of the numerous chairs rather than the sofa, Victoria forced a strained smile to her lips. "Mr. Humbly was just telling me of his intention to retire. It will be a sad loss."

"Very kind of you, my dear, but it shall be good for the church to have a new leader," Humbly retorted with admirable modesty. Then a rather sly glint entered his eyes. "It does not do to become mired in one path. A bit of change can be good for us all."

Victoria's smile faded. "Not all change is good."

The vicar shrugged. "It can certainly be disconcerting, but with a little effort, and of course a willingness to seek the best in a situation, it can usually be made into a good thing."

"Very wise words, Mr. Humbly," Claredon retorted, his fingers scrolling aimless patterns over Victoria's shivering skin. "To fight against the inevitable is always a wasted effort. Far better to take advantage of what is given."

She turned to offer her husband a glare that warned if his fingers strayed one inch lower she would break them, vicar or no vicar. "Even if one abhors what they are given?"

"Foolish dove," he chided, his blue eyes hardening with silent warning. "You shall have the good vicar believing you are speaking of your own situation, which would be absurd. Would it not?"

Aware that Humbly was indeed regarding her with a faint frown, she hurriedly sought to distract him. "Of course. Forgive me, Mr. Humbly. There have been times when the unexpected was not at all pleasant."

The older gentleman was swiftly contrite. "I am sorry, my dear. You speak, of course of your parents' sudden accident. Very clumsy of me. I did not mean to remind you of such a painful incident."

Her gaze lowered. It was not what she had been thinking of at all, but at the mention of her parents she felt a familiar hollowness in the pit of her stomach. She missed them, even more so during this turbulent time in her life. The pain of her wrenching loss had faded with time, but was never truly forgotten. "It is in the past," she said stiffly.

"But never far from your heart."

"I . . . no."

"You revealed remarkable courage in keeping your household from falling into ruin and raising your sister all alone," Humbly persisted, oddly not seeming to sense her reluctance in discussing that terrible time in her past. "Most young maidens never would have considered attempting such a feat, let alone have succeeded so admirably."

Victoria felt a heat crawl beneath her cheeks. "It was more necessity than courage."

"No." Humbly shook his head. "You could easily have handed your sister to a relative and requested that another handle the estate."

"I could not uproot poor Anna at such a time," she retorted in soft tones. "And to be honest, it was a blessing to have the estate matters to take my mind off my sadness."

Humbly was not about to be so easily put off. He had, of course, been close at hand to witness the struggle she had undertaken to convince the tenants to respect her opinion and the endless effort to keep the local merchants from attempting to use her inexperience to take advantage. He had, indeed, seen the days she was so weary of carrying the responsibilities of her parents that she could barely make it through the day.

"Say what you will, my dear, you could have turned your back on the burdens dumped upon you. Instead, you sacrificed your own life to ensure Anna's happiness."

Claredon's fingers abruptly tightened upon her shoulder, and Victoria uncomfortably realized that Humbly was revealing more of her past than she desired.

"Really, Mr. Humbly, it was what I desired to do. There was no sacrifice."

"Of course there was," he argued firmly. "But now Anna is safely wed, and it is the moment to think of yourself. That was why I was so anxious to assure myself that you are well."

Distinctly embarrassed by the undeserved praise,

Victoria shifted uneasily. "And now you know that everything has worked out perfectly," she muttered.

The vicar frowned at her words, not seemingly assured by her strained tones. "As you say."

Without warning, Claredon abruptly rose to his feet and with a determined air pulled Victoria to stand beside him.

"I believe Victoria is appearing a trifle worn," he said, an unnerving perception in those blue eyes. "If you will excuse us, I should have her tucked into bed."

The vicar struggled from his seat. "Yes, of course."

Putting an arm about Victoria's shoulders, Claredon gently steered her toward the door. "Come along, my dear."

For the first time in five months, Victoria did not argue.

Four

Claredon was disturbed.

Leading his wife down the corridor and toward the staircase, he covertly studied her elegant profile in the dim light.

He had, of course, known that her parents had been killed in a tragic carriage accident and that she possessed no close male relatives. But he had been unaware that she had been forced to shoulder such burdens at such a young age, burdens that surely would have made most maidens crumble in defeat.

There was no doubt he felt a large measure of pride in her strength of will. Unlike many gentlemen, he did not fear a woman of courage. Nor did he desire a mate who depended utterly upon him.

He admired in women precisely what he admired in men: Courage. Honor. Loyalty.

Three qualities that his wife possessed in abundance.

But while he readily conceded that Victoria had displayed rare determination to keep her sister and household together, he could not dismiss an odd flare of disappointment that she had never spoken of her trials. Surely as her husband he should know of such a difficult event in her life.

No doubt she readily unburdened her soul to her precious

Thomas Stice, a nasty voice whispered in the back of his mind. The mere thought was unpleasantly painful.

They climbed the stairs in silence, but as they moved toward her chambers, she abruptly tilted her head upward.

"It is not necessary to escort me to my door," she murmured

"I believe it is," he insisted, a frown drawing his brows together. "You were distinctly pale downstairs. Did the vicar upset you?"

There was a slight pause, and Claredon feared she might refuse to admit her distress. Then she gave a shrug. "It is always difficult to speak of my parents."

"Which, perhaps, explains your rather astonishing omission in telling me that you were forced to fend for yourself and your sister after their death."

He was unable to keep the edge from his voice, and her eyes widened in surprise.

"You knew I was in London to oversee my sister's launch into Society."

"I knew you had accompanied your sister to London," he corrected. "But I presumed Mrs. Stolden had charge of both of you."

"Aunt Millie?" She gave a startled laugh. "Good heavens, she came to us after my parents' deaths to lend us countenance, but she was hopeless to take command of anything beyond the daily menu."

His frown only deepened. "How old were you?"

"I was seventeen when my parents died."

"And your sister?"

"Fourteen."

A measure of anger surged through him at the thought of Victoria, so tenderly young and burdened with mourning for her parents, being forced to shoulder such responsibility.

Bloody hell. She should have had someone caring for her, someone who could have ensured she was safe and comfortable while she grieved for her loss. Someone who later ensured she could have the proper life for a young maiden. "So you never had a Season of your own?" he demanded.

She abruptly turned her head to hide her expressive features. "I never desired one."

He gave a disbelieving click of his tongue. "Not even before your parents died?"

"Really, Claredon, you cannot be interested in my youthful fantasies," she retorted in defensive tones.

"Oh, I am very interested," he countered, pulling open the door and stepping into her private chambers.

It was the first time he had been in her rooms, and Claredon was startled to discover the heavy English furnishings had been replaced with a delicate rosewood. Soft peach wall coverings were echoed in the flowered carpet and in the silk curtains, while upon the ceiling mischievous angels peeked from behind clouds. It was utterly feminine and not all what he had expected from his forceful wife.

The knowledge only reinforced his realization he knew very little of the woman who claimed his name. Firmly shutting the door, he leaned against it with a relentless expression. It was obviously past time for them to have a serious discussion. "I wish to know the truth," he said baldly.

Standing in the center of the room, Victoria eyed him warily. "The truth of what?"

"How did a maiden of seventeen take command of her own household?"

She looked as if she desired to command him to

leave her chamber, but clearly noting his determined air, she gave a frustrated shake of her head.

"As I told Mr. Humbly, it was simply a matter of necessity. After my parents were killed, there were few relatives willing to take in two young maidens. The few who tried to push their way forward were interested only in getting their hands upon our inheritance. Thankfully, the estate was not entailed and there was no title, so after I convinced Aunt Millie to claim guardianship, the vultures were turned aside. She is, after all, our closest relative."

Claredon thought of himself at the age of seventeen. He had still been in school and reckless to a fault. There had been few things more important than dice games, escaping the stern eye of the headmaster, and the pleasures of a particularly experienced barmaid.

How would he have reacted had his own parents died and he had been forced to take over as head of the family? He experienced a prick of dismay at the knowledge he could not be fully certain he would have possessed his wife's fortitude. He gave a restless shake of his head. "Surely there was someone you could depend upon?"

"I did not wish to depend upon anyone." Her chin tilted to a proud angle. "I was quite capable of taking care of both my sister and myself."

"Of course." He grimaced, all too familiar with that particular expression. On this occasion, however, he did not allow himself to bristle with the need to ruffle that rigid composure. Instead, he forced himself to consider how the tragedy in her life had molded her into such a powerful female. "I believe I at last begin to understand you, my dear."

Her gaze narrowed with suspicion at his mild tone. "What do you mean?"

"I now understand why you are such a strong-willed, managing female. You have been forced to take command and give orders to others."

An absurd expression of outrage rippled over her lovely countenance. "I am not a managing female."

He could not halt his laugh of disbelief. "My dear, you are perhaps the most ruthless bully I have ever encountered. There was not a gentleman in all of Society who was not terrified of you."

"That is absurd," she protested, her emerald eyes flashing. "And you are most certainly not terrified of me."

"No," he generously conceded, a sudden smile curving his lips. "But that is only because I am quite as stubborn and untrained to the bridle as yourself—which no doubt explains why we are constantly at daggers drawn."

As usual, she refused to concede she possessed any blame in their discomforting situation. Instead, she glared at him with a gathering anger. "We are at daggers drawn because you are arrogant to a fault and incessantly provoking."

Claredon remained unperturbed by her sharp words. He was beginning to suspect that they both deliberately used provoking words to keep a prickly distance between one another. Why they should feel the necessity to do so was a question he did not desire to ponder at the moment.

"And you are a sharp-tongued shrew," he retorted without rancor.

She planted her hands upon her hips. "I think you have said quite enough for one night."

"Ah, but I have not yet finished," he retorted, pushing away from the door to stroll toward her.

She stiffened as he halted a mere breath from her. For a moment, Claredon simply gazed at her delicate features.

He had known women far more beautiful, some who could make a gentleman halt in his tracks. But he did not think he had ever encountered a more fascinating countenance. Such an odd combination of stubborn determination and innocent vulnerability. And, of course, that enticing hint of sensuality that smoldered deep in her magnificent eyes and was evident in the lush curve of her lips.

His blood quickened as he realized he could never tire of studying those fine features. It spoke well of their future together.

With a visible effort, she forced herself not to retreat from his large form. "What is it?" she demanded.

"I also comprehend your fascination with Mr. Stice."

Her nose flared in protest at his smooth words. "You could never comprehend such pure emotion."

"Hardly pure," he corrected without apology. To be frank, he had endured enough of her absurd belief her feelings toward the namby-pamby twit were utterly superior to normal human emotions. No woman of intellect could think Mr. Stice the sort to inspire more than pity. "You were accustomed to playing the role of mother for your sister, and when she flew the nest, you swiftly sought to replace your missing chick. The hapless, rather pathetic Mr. Stice was the perfect choice."

His logical explanation was met with stony disbelief. Clearly she had not allowed herself to consider the notion she had been desperate to fill a suddenly empty place in her life, or that she had treated Mr. Stice more as a dutiful son than a lover.

"You could not be more in error," she at last said in flat tones. "I loved Thomas."

His heart twitched with what he swiftly assured himself was annoyance at her refusal to accept the truth. "Yes, as a mother loves her child," he said softly.

"No."

Damn, but she was stubborn. She would not even attempt to listen to reason. Then, abruptly recalling all she had endured and the courage she had displayed, his annoyance faded.

She had simply been in need of someone to love and care for, he reminded himself, and, at the time, clearly not in the position to have a child of her own.

Claredon stilled as inspiration struck with the force of a lightning bolt.

Of course.

Women such as Victoria would always need someone to fuss over. It was little wonder she appeared so restless and incapable of accepting her marriage.

"There is a very simple answer to your frustration," he murmured gently.

Her brows arched. "You intend to magically disappear from my life?" she demanded in overly sweet tones.

His eyes narrowed. "Have a child of your own."

A thick silence fell as she regarded him with disbelieving shock.

Claredon couldn't deny he was rather shocked himself. He had given little thought to siring children. It had not seemed necessary until he discovered the perfect woman.

Oddly, however, he discovered himself swiftly becoming accustomed to the notion. He did not doubt Victoria would be an excellent mother. And he had every intention of being a devoted father.

Why not begin a family?

Taking a sharp step backward, Victoria regarded him with an expression that warned him she was not nearly as accepting of the thought of creating a child as he was. "Good lord, do you never halt?" she at last managed to croak. "You will say and do anything to get into my bed. It is ridiculous."

The fact that he had for once been attempting to think of her needs threatened to stir his ever ready temper. He folded his arms across his chest and peered down the length of his nose. "You are not quite so irresistible as you believe, my dear. And I assure you that if I were that desperate to have you, I could easily have seduced you long ago."

Never able to leave well enough alone, she gave a toss of her head. "Not likely."

"It is a certainty." He closed the distance between them, reaching up to pluck the combs from her hair so the glossy tresses could tumble over her shoulders. "Shall I prove it here and now?"

Her lips parted as she battled the sudden crackle of heat in the air. Claredon was dangerously aware that she had never appeared lovelier, with her hair shimmering like fire in the candlelight, framing her softly flushed countenance, and the wide bed so conveniently near.

Far, far too near.

That delicious pulse at the base of her neck began its frantic pace, revealing that Victoria was far from indifferent to the fingers he allowed to brush softly over the line of her collarbone. "I want you out of my chambers," she said unsteadily.

He slowly smiled. "Frightened, Victoria?"

"Queasy," she brazenly lied. "The mere thought of you . . ."

Whatever insult she had been about to hurl was abruptly cut off by the simple process of covering her lips with his own.

For five months, she had denied the passion that pulsed between them. More than that, she had done her damnable best to imply he was as repulsive as the plague.

Really, enough was enough.

Not above using his rakish experience, Claredon deliberately softened his kiss, teasing her delectable lips until they parted and he was able to trace them lightly with the tip of his tongue.

He felt her shiver and swiftly wrapped his arms about her to pluck her close. His initial thought had been to halt her incessant rudeness, but his purpose was swiftly becoming lost in the pleasure swirling through him.

Bloody hell, but she felt good in his arms.

The softness of her curves fitted perfectly with the hardness of his own frame, her satin hair spilling over his hands and surrounding them in lilac heat. And those lips. Those lush, sensuous lips that would provoke a saint to madness.

A madness that was swiftly consuming him. A difficult admission for a gentleman renowned for always being in control of the fine art of seduction—difficult and a bit alarming.

Pulling back, he regarded her flushed countenance with an unwittingly brooding gaze. "A word of advice, my love," he said in husky tones. "Never challenge a gentleman's prowess as a lover. It makes him quite determined to prove his worth."

A spark of panic glittered in her emerald eyes. "Let me go."

"In a moment."

"Claredon."

"You are quite breathtaking, you know," he husked softly, his gaze unable to leave her delicately tinted features. "Hair the color of a blazing sunset, eyes as rich as emeralds, and that skin. That enticing, silken skin."

For a moment, she appeared as spellbound as he. Then, with an effort, she forced herself to recall she did not particularly like him. "I want you to leave."

He cast a regretful glance toward the bed. "You are certain?"

"Yes."

With great deal more reluctance than he cared to admit, Claredon dropped his arms and stepped back. He had not, however, given up on his clever notion. "Think upon what I have said, Victoria. You are lonely and in need of someone to devote your heart to. A child could bring you happiness."

She pushed back her heavy curls with a hand that was not quite steady. "This is just another means of attempting to seduce me."

He gave a dry laugh. "Actually, for once I am truly thinking of you. I had not realized how much you have been forced to sacrifice. I admire your strength and wish to give you some means of happiness."

Something that might have been pain darkened her eyes. "And yourself a willing lover who is conveniently close at hand."

"Why are you so reluctant to admit that you desire me?" he demanded with a hint of impatience. "We are wed. There is nothing shameful in enjoying the touch of your husband."

"I have told you, I will not be another conquest."

He reached out to brush her chin upward. "You desire me to swear I will be faithful only to you?"

"I would never ask the impossible," she retorted, hastily backing from his touch.

"Once again, you are quite off the mark."

"You are saying you would never take a mistress if I allowed you into my bed?"

He smiled wryly at her disbelief. There were times his reputation was a deuced nuisance. "I am saying that I vowed to be faithful the day we wed."

Her breath caught. "Ridiculous."

"Why?"

"I . . . you have always had a mistress."

"Not always," he denied, holding her gaze with his own. "And never when I possessed a wife."

She gave a slow shake of her head. "And you wish me to believe that a wife will make a difference to you?"

"It makes all the difference." With an effort, Claredon battled to maintain his patience. She wanted to believe the worst in him. It would be up to him to teach her that he was more than a scandalous rogue—always supposing he did not strangle her first. "Regardless of the unfortunate reason for our marriage, you are now my wife. Your position demands my respect, and I would do nothing to bring embarrassment to you."

Her fierce expression briefly faltered with uncertainty. "It is hardly uncommon for a husband to seek pleasure outside his home."

Claredon winced as he recalled his own father's peccadilloes. He had certainly never taken care to hide his infidelities, nor even to spare a thought for his wife left at home. It was not that he was a cruel man. He merely presumed his behavior was that of any other noble gentleman.

"Perhaps not," he admitted in low tones. "But after witnessing my mother's distress when my father flaunted his birds of paradise, I made a personal decision never to bring such shame to my own family. As much as I love my father, I have never forgiven him for hurting my mother."

A thick silence descended as she regarded him with an unreadable expression. Claredon prepared himself for her condemning words. He had never before revealed his deeply hidden disappointment in his father, and he was all too aware his wife possessed no trust in him.

Would she consider this yet another ploy to seduce her?

The silence lengthened then, just when he was prepared to toss up his hands in defeat, she allowed her features to soften. "I am sorry."

Caught off guard by her low words, he regarded her with a lift of his brows. "For what?"

"I know you are very attached to your father," she explained with a troubled expression. "That was why I . . ."

"Why you what?" he prompted.

"Why I assumed you would be willing to follow his example."

Claredon breathed in deeply, realizing that there had been a great deal too much assumption on both sides.

"Perhaps you could have spoken to me rather than simply having presumed the worst?" he said with a wry smile.

"You have never indicated that you consider our marriage as anything more than a rather poor jest."

He acknowledged her hit with a bow of his head, well aware he had walked into her thrust like a simpleton. "Neither one of us have attempted to put our best foot forward."

"No," she breathed.

"Maybe we should consider the vicar's words."

"What words?"

"Of attempting to seek out the best in our situation. We are, after all, stuck with one another."

An indefinable emotion darkened her emerald eyes before she abruptly spun away. "It is not so simple."

Claredon swallowed an impatient sigh as he ran his hand through his dark hair. Blast it all, she was as stubborn as an ox. "You would prefer that we devote the next fifty-odd years to sniping at one another and making ourselves miserable?" he demanded.

"Of course not." Her head bowed with an oddly vulnerable motion. "But I cannot just dismiss the fact we are little more than strangers forced into this situation because you wished to seduce my own cousin."

Claredon stiffened, refusing to take the full blame for their damnable situation. "Or if you had not heedlessly been eloping with an incompetent fool while masquerading as your cousin," he retorted stiffly. "If you will recall, there were two of us in that bed."

She shuddered, but refused to turn about and face him. "Did you love her?"

"What?"

"My cousin. Did you love her?"

"Good lord, no," he protested with a grimace at the mere thought of Lady Westfield. The beautiful but coldly predatory woman was a danger to gentlemen everywhere. It was incredible that she was even related to Victoria, no matter how remotely. "Indeed, I have been battling her attempts at seduction for the past year."

She gave a choked laugh. "Forgive me if I find that rather difficult to believe."

He batted the urge to shake her. He was unaccustomed to having to explain himself to anyone, let alone an innocent chit who knew nothing of the meaningless games played between the more jaded members of the *ton*.

"If you must know the sordid truth, I thought she had followed me from London," he grudgingly revealed, discovering he was not entirely proud of his actions upon that fateful evening. "It certainly would not have been the first occasion she had done such a thing. Once she even possessed the audacity to slip into my town house through the servant's entrance. Since I had no desire to have her following me around the countryside, I had hoped that by offering her what she obviously wished for, she would leave me in peace."

She slowly turned to regard him with a startled expression. "Oh."

His lips twisted. It was not a simple matter to discuss his scandalous behavior with a true innocent. To be frank, he was beginning to feel a bit guilty—which was absurd, of course. "Have I shocked you, my dear?"

Her lips thinned with disapproval. "I do not comprehend how you can be so casual about such matters."

He gave a slow shake of his head as he stepped toward her. He would not have her thinking he considered her just another female. She was his wife, his mate for life. "There is nothing casual in my response to you, Victoria," he promised in low tones. "I do not believe I have ever had a woman haunt me with such frustrating persistence."

Her tongue peeked out to wet her lips in a nervous manner. "No doubt because no other woman has ever bothered to resist your advances."

"Ah, no, it is more than that. I . . ." His soft words of seduction were rudely interrupted as a distant cry echoed through the air. With a frown he glanced toward the door. "What the devil was that?"

"It sounded like Vicar Humbly," she retorted, moving with astonishing speed to wrench open the door and disappear down the hall.

On his own, Claredon tossed his hands up in surrender.

He could only presume he was being punished for his very long list of sins. Why else would he have been saddled with the one woman in all of England he could not seduce? It truly was an astonishing irony.

"Bloody hell," he muttered, moving to follow his maddening wife.

Five

After nearly sixty years upon earth, few things managed to startle Vicar Humbly.

He had once been shot at when he had come too close to a gang of smugglers. He had been forced to deliver a baby in the middle of a church service. He had even had a widow desperate for a husband slip into his chambers late one evening.

But the surprisingly worldly vicar could not deny a decided flare of shock when he entered the library to discover a man crawling through the window.

Coming to a startled halt, the vicar called out before he could halt himself.

Not surprisingly, the intruder had briefly frozen in horror at being discovered. Then, with astonishing speed, he was shoving himself back out of the window and disappearing into the night.

Belatedly realizing the scoundrel was escaping, Humbly hurried across the room to peer out the window.

Blast!

He never should have alerted the intruder he was aware of his presence. Instead, he should have quietly backed out of the room and sought out a couple of burly footmen to apprehend the villain.

Now it was far too late.

Muttering at his stupidity, Humbly turned and discovered Victoria hurrying through the open door with a worried expression.

"Vicar Humbly, what is it?" she demanded. "Have you had an accident?"

Unaware that his shout had carried throughout the household, Humbly gave an embarrassed grimace. "No, no. Forgive me for creating such a fuss," he murmured as he moved toward the young maiden. "I feel very foolish."

She frowned with obvious suspicion. "Something must have occurred."

"Yes," agreed a dark male voice as Claredon stepped into the room to stand beside his wife. "What is it, Humbly?"

Humbly briefly debated within himself. He had no desire to worry Claredon or Victoria unnecessarily. After all, he was wise enough to realize that their marriage was not nearly as satisfactory as they desired him to believe. He was not such a fool as to miss the prickly antagonism that lay thick in the air between them, nor Victoria's near panic when her husband touched her. It was obvious that they needed to concentrate on building a future, rather than brooding upon regrets of the past. He did not wish them to be distracted by this unfortunate incident.

Then again, he realized that Claredon had every right to know his home had been invaded. Who knew what harm the villain had been intent upon? He could not in all conscience allow the household to be placed in danger because of his silence.

Heaving a sigh of regret that he was adding yet more troubles to poor Victoria, he absently patted his renegade strands of hair. "Yes, well, I had gone to my room to retire for the night when I recalled that

I had left my watch in the library. Hardly an unusual occurrence, I fear. I am always leaving it about somewhere. Devilish inconvenient, I assure you."

"Yes, I can imagine," Claredon said with forced patience. "You were about to tell us why you cried out."

"Of course." Humbly smiled with apology at his rambling. "As I said, I left my watch, so I decided to return to the library to retrieve it while I could still recall where it was. But I had just entered the room when I spotted a gentleman entering through the window."

"What?" Victoria gasped in shock, even as Claredon swiftly crossed the room to study the still open window.

"I must say I was too startled to think clearly," Humbly admitted. "Now I realize I should have gone in search of a servant to nab the thief, rather than calling out and frightening him away."

Victoria pressed a hand to her heart. "Good heavens, you believe him to be a thief?"

"This lock has definitely been forced," Claredon announced from across the room.

"But why?" Victoria gave a shake of her head. "What could a thief desire?"

Claredon straightened, his features set in grim lines. "It is difficult to say. Having so recently restored the estate, there are few objects of value. Most of my collection of art and rare manuscripts are still in my London town house. And, of course, the Moreland jewels remain in my mother's possession."

"Perhaps the silver or the china your parents gave us upon our wedding?" Victoria suggested without much confidence.

"Or perhaps the thief simply did not realize you were so new to the neighborhood," Humbly added.

Claredon gave a shake of his head as he closed the

window. Obviously he was not reassured by the half-hearted explanations. Humbly had to admit he found them rather implausible as well.

"It still does not make sense," Claredon retorted as he paced back across the room. "Why would any thief chose this small estate when there are others far more grand within an easy distance? Or why, for that matter, would they chose to enter while we were at home?"

Humbly gave a lift of his hands. "I suppose desperation could lead a man to actions not readily comprehensible to others. 'Hope deferred makes the heart sick, but a desire fulfilled is a tree of life.'"

Claredon appeared thoroughly unsympathetic. Indeed, there was a dangerous glitter in those blue eyes that sent a cold chill down the vicar's spine. He would not like to be the poor fool who dared to anger Lord Claredon.

"Can you recall anything of the intruder?" Claredon demanded in clipped tones.

Rather unnerved by his piercing gaze, the vicar attempted to form the image of the man he had so briefly glimpsed. Not an easy task, considering he had been decidedly rattled at the time.

"Let me think," he muttered. "He was young. Not much older than Victoria, I would guess. He had a thin countenance and rather light brown hair."

"And what of his form? Was he tall or short?"

Humbly gave an apologetic shake of his head, regretting that he had not taken better note of the stranger. "I really cannot say. He was only half through the window when I inadvertently frightened him away. And what I did see was covered by a black cape."

"A cape?" Claredon demanded sharply.

Uncertain why a cape would startle the younger gentleman, Humbly gave a slow nod of his head. "Yes. A satin cape."

"Hardly the normal attire of a common ruffian, I would think."

"No," Humbly agreed, at last comprehending Claredon's surprise. What desperate criminal could afford a satin cape? Such a man was far more likely to be attired in rough clothing than clothes fit for an evening at the opera.

"What is it?" Victoria demanded with a frown.

"Now that I think upon it, he had more the appearance of a nobleman than a commoner," Humbly confessed in thoughtful tones.

"This grows more odd by the moment," Claredon growled. "Can you think of nothing that would help us to recognize him?"

Readily agreeing that it was indeed odd, Humbly searched his mind for a means of being of service. Unfortunately, he could think of nothing out of the ordinary to offer.

"It is very difficult to describe a face with words."

"Wait. I have an idea," Victoria abruptly said. "I shall return in a moment."

Without giving either gentleman an opportunity to protest, Victoria dashed from the room. Although startled by the maiden's sudden departure, Humbly did not miss the manner in which Claredon stepped toward the door, as if reluctant to have his wife out of his sight.

Humbly swiftly hid a smile of satisfaction. He discovered that unconscious display of protection far more convincing of Claredon's feelings toward his wife than the deliberate displays of affection he had been offered since his arrival.

The gentleman might not yet realize his feelings for Victoria, but Humbly was suddenly reassured that they did exist, no matter how reluctantly.

They waited in tense silence for Victoria's return. Humbly covertly studied the taut lines of Lord Claredon's countenance as he restlessly prowled the room.

Within moments Victoria rushed back through the door, carrying a sketchpad and small piece of charcoal. She moved directly to the desk, where she pulled out a clean sheet of paper.

"What are you doing?" Claredon demanded with a puzzled frown.

"We shall create a face that can be recognized," she said simply, turning her attention toward Humbly. "Now, Vicar, tell me again his features. You said that his countenance was thin. Was it thinner than Claredon's?"

Intrigued by Victoria's notion, Humbly moved to stand behind her chair, peering over her shoulder as she made a few bold lines upon the page.

"Yes," he agreed, dredging up the vague memories of the intruder. "And longer, with a pointed chin."

"And his nose?"

For nearly half an hour, Victoria ruthlessly quizzed him on each feature, until, after nearly a dozen different sketches, Humbly was satisfied she had managed to capture the basic image of the stranger.

"There," he at last pronounced, holding the sketch in his hand. "This is very close."

Standing at his side, Claredon smiled at his wife in a rather startled manner. "Very clever, my dear."

A hint of warmth touched Victoria's cheeks as she rose to her feet. "We shall be able to use the sketch to question the servants and tenants. Perhaps they have noticed such a gentleman in the neighborhood."

"Yes." The smile faded as Claredon's expression hardened with determination. "I would very much like to have a word with our intruder."

Victoria cast her husband a worried glance, as if sensing he was prepared to go to any lengths to discover the stranger. "But not tonight, I think," she said firmly.

He paused, as if reluctant to concede there was nothing he could accomplish in the dead of night. At last he gave a rueful shrug.

"No, it is rather late. You should go up to bed, my dear."

"Yes." Victoria gave an absent nod. "Good night."

She turned to move toward the door, and Humbly hid a smile as Claredon swiftly followed in her wake.

"Victoria." He halted her as she prepared to slip through the door.

Turning, she regarded him in puzzlement. "Yes?"

His hand reached to gently cradle her cheek as he bent to brush his lips over her forehead. "Lock your door."

She appeared too startled to protest his soft command and with a flustered expression hurried down the hall.

Watching the tender exchange, Humbly slowly smiled.

It appeared Victoria at long last possessed a champion determined to protect her.

Unaware of the vicar's scrutiny, Claredon watched as his wife scurried toward the shadowed stairs. It took a great deal of effort to allow her to be out of his sight.

He had been badly shaken by the knowledge some

villain had attempted to creep into his home. Not that he was frightened for himself. He had always kept himself in good shape and was as proficient with his fists as he was with a pistol. Any scoundrel attempting to best him would swiftly discover that he had taken on more than he had bargained for.

But the realization that Victoria had been in danger made his blood rush in fury. What if Victoria had walked in on the intruder? What if he had managed to slip into her room undetected?

What if . . .

The potential disasters raced through his thoughts with an alarming speed. In all his life, he had never been responsible for another, and he was discovering a fiercely protective instinct stirred to life he never dreamed that he possessed.

It was rather frightening just how acutely painful the thought of Victoria in danger was to him, and how deadly determined he was to bring an end to that danger.

Abruptly turning on his heel, Claredon crossed toward the mahogany sideboard. "I believe I can use a drink. What of you, Humbly?" he asked in tight tones.

"Yes, a brandy would be most welcome," the vicar readily agreed.

Pouring two generous measures of the brandy, Claredon moved to hand Humbly a glass, then drained his own with one swallow. The heat of the fine spirit helped to ease the cold fury that gripped him, and he offered the vicar a rueful smile. "A most astonishing evening for you, eh, Humbly?"

"As you say, most astonishing," the older gentleman said as he sipped the brandy. "It gave me quite a turn to walk in and discover a man dangling from the window."

"Yes, I can imagine."

"I do wish, however, I had kept my wits about me," he admitted with a sigh. "If I had not called out, we might easily have caught him."

Claredon gave a wave of his hand. Certainly he would have preferred to have captured the scoundrel the moment he stepped foot upon the grounds, but he did not blame the poor vicar for his instinctive alarm. "Nonsense. Had the villain actually been allowed to enter the house, we have no notion what he might have done. If he were armed, it would have been very difficult to overpower him."

Obviously reassured, Mr. Humbly gave a nod of his head. "Yes, I suppose."

"I am only relieved you were not injured."

Without warning, the vicar gave a sudden chuckle. "To be honest, I believe he appeared as frightened and startled as I when I entered the room."

Claredon gave a slow nod of his head. "An amateur, then."

"That would be my guess."

"It still makes no sense." Claredon set his glass upon the desk with a sharp bang. He did not like the nagging sensation that there was more to this stranger than he could put his finger upon. "Whether the intruder was an amateur or not, he must have realized that the servants would be moving through the house extinguishing the candles and checking the fireplaces."

"A mystery, indeed," Humbly agreed in sympathetic tones. "Perhaps Victoria's sketching will help us discover his identity."

Claredon cast a glance toward the sketch the vicar had left lying upon the desk. He experienced an odd flare of pride in his wife's sensible approach to discovering the thief. Unlike many maidens, she had not been thrown into the vapors or taken to her bed at learning a stranger had attempted to enter the house. Instead, she had calmly offered her assistance with an enviable presence of mind.

"Yes," he murmured. "I intend to take it to the tenants tomorrow and then the village. If he is staying locally, then we will track him down."

"A very clever notion of Victoria to draw his sketch."

An unwitting smile curved Claredon's lips. "Victoria is always clever."

The vicar polished off his brandy and set the glass aside. "I do hope she will not be overset by the disturbance."

Claredon gave a lift of his brows. "Victoria? I do not believe I have seen my wife overset by anything," he retorted, only to realize that he was not being entirely honest. That fateful night she had awakened to discover herself in his arms, she had been decidedly overset. So overset her screams had brought everyone in the posting inn to her door. "Well, perhaps once."

With an astute swiftness that was generally hidden beneath his vague air, the vicar gave a sudden cough. "Yes, quite," he said, fussing with his sadly crumpled cravat. "She is not a highly strung maiden. Very fortunate, of course, considering the trials she has been forced to bear."

Claredon could not prevent a wry smile at the mumbled words. "Am I to be considered one of her trials?"

The older gentleman possessed the grace to blush at the blunt question. "Actually, I refer more to the events that led to your marriage," he was hasty to reassure.

Claredon gave a restless shrug, not overly eager to discuss his marriage with the vicar. He did not share Victoria's confidence that they could manage to hide the near state of warfare they lived in. "It was unfortunate, but we have accepted the situation," he reluctantly lied.

The sherry eyes narrowed in an unnerving manner. "Have you?"

"As well as possible."

A taut silence descended before Humbly gently cleared his throat. "Forgive me for prying, but was there another you wished to wed?"

The gentleman's perception caught Claredon off guard and before he could halt himself he had already given a nod of his head. "Oh, yes."

"I see. I am sorry."

Feeling a fool for having revealed his very private hopes for the future, Claredon gave a sharp shake of his head. He could not allow the vicar to believe he was nursing a broken heart. Only broken dreams. "Do not be sorry. I had not yet discovered her."

Not surprisingly, the vicar's plump countenance registered bewildered confusion. "I beg your pardon?"

Knowing he was bound to appear a ready candidate for Bedlam, Claredon heaved a sigh. "She was merely in my mind," he reluctantly confessed. "I have always harbored an image of the perfect maiden I would one day wed."

"I see," the vicar at last murmured, leaving Claredon with the uncomfortable sensation that perhaps he did see. All too well. "I did not realize that there had ever been a perfect maiden."

Claredon curbed his flare of impatience toward the kindly man. "I meant perfect for me."

"Ah." A rather mysterious twinkle entered the

sherry eyes. "And what sort of woman would that be?"

Claredon did not trust that twinkle, nor the unmistakable sense that there was more than a trace of amusement in his tone.

"Kind. Courageous. Loyal. Intelligent," he forced himself to retort in a tight voice. No one could possibly comprehend his desire to discover that woman he had nourished deep in his heart—or his reason for seeking her in the first place. "It also would have been nice if she possessed a sense of humor."

Humbly gave a lift of his brows. "And you have never encountered a maiden who possessed such qualities?"

"As I am sure you are aware, I have devoted little attention to encountering proper maidens," he retorted dryly. "There had always seemed ample time to acquire a wife."

There was a deliberate pause before Humbly slowly smiled. "It seems to me that despite the circumstances of your marriage, you managed to wed precisely the sort of woman you desired."

Claredon stilled at the soft words.

Victoria the woman he had dreamed of for so many years?

Ridiculous, of course.

She was stubborn, sharp tongued, and ill tempered. She was also bitterly resentful at being forced to become his wife. Not anything at all like the sweet, lovingly gentle maiden he had hoped to discover.

Still, he could not entirely deny that the vicar had a legitimate argument.

Victoria did possess courage and loyalty and a shrewd intelligence. She was also beautiful and utterly desirable, if only she would lower her prickly barriers. He could certainly have done considerably worse, he acknowledged with a grudging smile.

"I suppose," he murmured, not at all prepared to claim Victoria as his perfect mate.

Not as long as she was making him batty.

Easily seeing through his less than enthusiastic agreement, Humbly regarded him with a piercing gaze. "Of course, I would imagine that marriage in the beginning is difficult for all couples, especially when it was not precisely what either of you desired."

Claredon nearly choked at the absurd understatement. His marriage to Victoria had not been difficult, it had been bloody impossible. "You have no notion."

"Perhaps I have a small notion," the vicar surprisingly insisted. "You see, I had no desire to become a vicar."

Unable to make the leap between his marriage and choosing whether or not to become a vicar, Claredon gave a faint frown. Perhaps the old boy was a bit more noddy than he had realized. "No?"

"Certainly not," Humbly retorted with seemingly sane sincerity. "Being a vicar always seemed such dull work with few rewards, and, of course, it was hardly a career that made the maidens swoon with delight. I was quite set upon joining the military. There are few things more dashing than a gentleman in his regimentals."

Claredon felt his lips twitch in spite of himself. The mere thought of the rotund, rumpled vicar in regimentals was decidedly ludicrous. "I presume you had a change of heart?"

"No, my father simply refused to consider purchasing me a commission." Humbly heaved a reminiscent sigh. "He also refused to support any other feather-brained scheme I might harbor. I was to become a vicar, or I would be cut off entirely from my family."

Having been decidedly spoiled by his own father, Claredon could not help but experience a flare of surprise. "A rather harsh ultimatum."

The vicar grimaced. "Yes. And I will admit I was decidedly resentful for a goodly time."

"Any young gentleman would be."

That unnerving glint returned to his eyes. "It took far too long for me to realize my resentment of losing my dream was harming no one but myself. I had accepted my father's demands rather than striking out on my own, and it was upon my own shoulders to make something good of my choice or give sway to bitterness."

Claredon smiled with cynical amusement at the vicar's less than subtle jab. He did not doubt the wily old fox was referring directly to his marriage with Victoria. "You make is sound very simple."

He shrugged. "It was once I accepted my path was destined to travel a direction I had not anticipated."

"And you have no regrets?" Claredon demanded in disbelief.

"Of course. I should have appeared very handsome in regimentals," Humbly retorted with a sweet smile. "In the end, however, I am satisfied that I have been the very best vicar I knew how to be. There is a great deal of satisfaction in that. Now I will bid you good night. I believe I have had enough excitement for one day."

With a faint bow, the vicar turned to make his way from the room.

Claredon watched his retreat with a narrowed gaze. Despite his prick of annoyance at being gently chastised by the older gentleman, he could not deny that there had been a great deal of sense in Humbly's words. His path had irrevocably been altered the day he had wed Victoria. It was past time he laid his childish fantasy aside and the regret he would never know his dream maiden.

It was the only means of allowing room for Victoria in his heart.

Six

It took a considerable amount of courage for Victoria to leave her bedchamber the next morning.

Despite her grim determination to banish all thoughts of Claredon from her mind, she had spent a long, sleepless night recalling his absurd accusations.

How dare he imply her love for Thomas was that of a mother for her child? Granted, Thomas was of a far gentler, more easily swayed nature than Claredon. And their love was more one of friendship than passion. But that did not mean she had simply attached herself to him out of some odd desire to have someone to mother.

It was all utterly ridiculous.

So why had she twisted and turned throughout the long night?

Was it because his talk of children has stirred to life a deep ache of loneliness she had tried so desperately to bury? Because he had forced her to truly consider the notion that they were tied to one another forever? Because he promised he would be a faithful husband? Because for just one moment when he had held her in his arms, she had not wanted him to let her go?

They were troublesome thoughts that she possessed no desire to ponder.

Instead, she had risen from her bed and sternly turned her mind toward the strange intruder who had attempted to sneak into Longmeade. No doubt Claredon had already begun his search for the culprit, and while a childish part of her longed to remain in her chamber and hide from the disturbing companionship of her husband, the more sensible side of her nature realized she should offer her assistance.

This was her home as well as Claredon's, and she had no intention of allowing villains to waltz in and out of her windows. With that thought firmly in the forefront of her mind, she had gone in search of Claredon.

It came as rather a surprise to discover he was not at all anxious to allow her to accompany him as he questioned the tenants or when he was preparing to travel to the village to speak with the local merchants. He ridiculously claimed it was his responsibility to protect his household. Only because she was quite as stubborn as he did he grudgingly allow her to ride in the carriage with him.

Really, she stewed as she awaited his return from the posting inn, one would think he suspected that the entire countryside was littered with dangerous rogues. For a woman unaccustomed to anyone concerning themselves with her welfare, it was a decidedly odd sensation to suddenly be treated as if she were a delicate object.

Odd and not entirely unpleasant, a traitorous voice whispered in the back of her mind.

Not that she intended ever to allow Claredon to order her about or to dictate what she could or could not do, she swiftly assured herself. But there was something rather nice about having someone who actually considered her as a vulnerable woman rather than the invincible Victoria.

With a shake of her head at her ridiculous fancies, Victoria peered through the window toward the bustling posting inn. The mild summer weather had shifted overnight, bringing in a gray drizzle that blanketed the small village. Through the tenacious tentacles of fog Victoria at last spotted the tall, elegant form of her husband.

A strangely familiar tingle of recognition inched down her spine as he neared, as if her body possessed a special connection to him that went beyond her rational mind.

It was a recognition she had realized early in her marriage and why she had so determinedly fought his seduction. She might not be able to control the unruly response of her body, but she was wise enough to know that passion without love would be a shallow affair.

With a fluid grace, Claredon stepped into the carriage and closed the door behind him. He carefully removed his wet coat and set it on the opposite seat before lowering himself beside her.

"Well?" she demanded impatiently, as much to distract herself from the warm clean scent of him as to discover what had occurred in the inn.

Surprisingly, a satisfied smile curved his lips. "Success at last."

Victoria widened her eyes in astonishment. "Someone recognized the sketch?"

"The innkeep. He said the man arrived two days ago and signed in as Frank Smith."

Victoria shivered. Perhaps ridiculously, the knowledge this man had been recognized was rather disturbing. Suddenly he was no longer a vague form conjured by Vicar Humbly, but a flesh and blood villain boldly residing at the local inn.

"Hardly original," she muttered.

"No, he does not appear to be a very clever criminal."

"But what could he possibly desire?"

"That is what I intend to discover."

There was a dangerous edge to his voice that brought a frown to Victoria's brow. "What are you going to do?"

As if sensing her concern, Claredon gave a dismissive shrug. "The innkeep noted Mr. Smith slipping out of the inn earlier this morning. He will eventually have to return, and I intend to be waiting for him."

Victoria gave an instinctive shake of her head at the notion of her husband so openly exposing himself to the criminal. "I do not think that is wise."

His brows raised in surprise at her sharp tone. "Why?"

"He could be dangerous."

An undeniable emotion rippled over his countenance before he offered her a reassuring smile. "I will await him in the public rooms. There is little he can do if surrounded by others."

"You cannot be certain."

He regarded her for a long, silent moment before slowly shaking his head. "You surprise me, Victoria."

"Why?"

"I should have thought it would suit you very well to have me conveniently disposed of."

Victoria's momentary shock was swiftly replaced by a flood of fury at his carefully bland words. "How dare you accuse me of something so horrid?" she breathed in shaken tones.

He grimaced, his hand reaching out to cover her clenched fist. "Forgive me, that was unkind."

She abruptly dropped her gaze to where his hand engulfed her own. She was angry and oddly hurt he would think her capable of such a ghastly desire. "I would not wish harm upon anyone."

"Of course you would not," he said in low tones. "I did not truly believe you would, but I fear a gentleman's pride can be an unpredictable thing."

Her head lifted at his baffling explanation. "What?"

"Never mind." He gave her hand a gentle squeeze. "It is time for you to return to Longmeade."

"Without you?" she demanded, her frown returning as she recalled his determination to confront the thief.

"I will have Johnson drive you home and return to fetch me later."

She unconsciously squared her shoulders in determination. "No, you cannot stay here on your own."

"I have assured you there will be no danger."

"Then allow me to remain," she swiftly countered.

His hand lifted to softly brush a curl that had escaped from beneath her bonnet. "Victoria, you cannot remain in the public room."

"Then I will remain here in the carriage," she retorted, attempting to ignore the sheer pleasure of his fingers as they trailed over her cheek. "If I spot the man entering the inn, I can send in a groom to warn you."

He was shaking his head before she had even finished speaking. "And if he manages to recognize the carriage, he will most certainly bolt."

Victoria heaved an annoyed sigh at his logical arguments. Blast it all, she would not allow him to expose himself to such danger. "I do not want you staying here alone," she said in tones that warned him she would not budge.

A rather worrisome smile played about his mouth before he gave a slow nod of his head. "Very well. I will have the groom remain with me."

"And you will be careful," she demanded.

"I will take the utmost care." Holding her worried gaze, he bent his head downward.

Victoria knew he was about to kiss her. She also knew that he was allowing her ample opportunity to halt his advance.

But she made no effort to avoid the lips that softly covered her own, not even when they deepened the kiss to reveal a rigidly restrained hunger that was echoed deep within her.

For long, dizzying moments, they both became lost in the swift, relentless need that burned to sudden life.

The cramped carriage, the rain peppering against the windows, the nearby servants all faded as wicked temptation swirled through the air. It was at last the shout of a coachman as a carriage entered the yard that intruded upon their spell of bewitchment.

Reluctantly pulling back, Claredon silently considered her flushed features for a long moment before ruefully dropping a soft kiss upon her nose and reaching for his coat.

With swift movements, he stepped out of the carriage and gave his commands to the waiting coachman. "Take Lady Claredon home, and then return and await me beyond the blacksmith's."

"Very good, my lord."

"Peter will remain here with me."

"Yes, sir."

There was a moment's pause as the groom climbed

from the carriage. Then, at a nod from Claredon, the waiting horses were set into motion.

Victoria barely noted as they swept from the yard and turned onto the road that eventually led to Longmeade. Instead she lingered in the fog of sensations that Claredon's touch had so easily seduced to life. With a hesitant movement, her fingers lifted to touch the lips that still throbbed from his kiss.

No, it was much more than a mere kiss, she grudgingly conceded. Thomas had kissed her, wet seeking lips that had only made her wish for the moment to be done. Claredon had bewitched her.

His lips created magic, his touch utter pleasure. Most worrying of all, however, was the tenderness that called to her wary heart. Against her will, his words of the evening before floated through her mind.

I vowed to be faithful the day we wed . . .

Was it possible he did intend to be true to her? That he was genuinely determined to build a relationship between them? Or were his promises the words of a practiced seducer who knew best how to tempt her?

Did she trust him?

Did she desire to trust him?

A faint frown marred her brow. She was far from certain she was prepared to consider the questions. It implied she was prepared to accept Claredon as a part of her life, and that she had forgiven him for ruining her plans for a marriage with Thomas.

Her hand dropped back into her lap as she heaved a sigh. Perhaps it would be better to consider such weighty matters when she was not still tingling with the pleasurable heat of his caresses, she acknowledged wryly.

The carriage slowed and, with a faint frown, Victoria peered out the window to discover they had just passed the small church and were entering the vast woods that framed Longmeade's parkland.

Opening the window she watched as the coachman climbed down from his seat.

"What is it, Johnson?" she demanded.

"There is a branch across the road, my lady. I shall have it cleared in a moment."

Closing the window, she settled back into the leather squabs. She knew better than to offer her services to the proud Johnson. He would be deeply shocked at the mere thought of her dampening her soft kid half boots. The staff had a very peculiar notion of what was proper for Lady Claredon, despite the fact she had often pitched in wherever needed at her own estate.

She had barely managed to rearrange her skirts when the door to the carriage was abruptly pulled open. Presuming Johnson had reluctantly overcome his qualms to request her help, Victoria leaned forward, only to come to a startled halt when a large form abruptly blocked the opening.

This was not her servant, she instantly recognized, although she noted little more than a black hat pulled low over a thin countenance nearly hidden by a black scarf. Her attention was riveted upon the deadly pistol the stranger had pointed straight at her heart.

Feeling as if she had stumbled into some horrid nightmare, Victoria could do no more than gape in shock as the man leaned toward her.

"You have my jewels," he rasped in a low whisper. "Bring them to the church at midnight tonight. Come alone or die."

"Jewels?" she managed to croak, but it was too late. The stranger abruptly whirled about, his cape billowing like a shadow behind him.

Shaken by the unexpected encounter, Victoria desperately attempted to gather her wits.

Blast! The villain was getting away and she had done nothing to halt him or even to discover his identity.

Cursing her ridiculous flare of fear, she bent forward, intent on at least discovering the direction the villain was fleeing. Her view, however, was swiftly blocked as Johnson came puffing to the door, his expression concerned.

"My lady, are you harmed?" he demanded in broken tones.

"No, I am fine," she swiftly assured the coachman.

"I did not realize . . . I am sorry, my lady. I should not have left you on your own."

Realizing that the faithful servant was swiftly working himself into a torrent of self-incrimination, Victoria forced a calmness to her countenance that she was far from feeling. "Do not be absurd. You could not have known the scoundrel was lurking about," she said in firm tones. "I believe, however, we should continue to Longmeade so that you can return and warn Lord Claredon of the danger."

"Yes, my lady. At once."

Clearly relieved to have tangible duties to take his thoughts off his failure to protect her, Johnson closed the door to the carriage and clambered back onto his seat.

With a crack of the whip, they were off, and Victoria drew in a shaky breath.

The stranger was obviously a madman, she acknowledged, as a chill crept down her spine. To

actually have stopped the carriage in broad daylight
and pointed a gun at her heart . . .

Yes, most definitely a madman.

And a dangerous one at that.

Sprawled in a dark corner of the public room, from
beneath the lowered rim of his hat, Claredon kept a
careful eye upon the various guests streaming into the
room. He had ordered his groom to lounge about the
stables to ensure the man did not attempt to slip to his
rooms through the servants' entrance.

When the thief returned to the inn he would have
him, Claredon thought with a flare of satisfaction.

A good thing, too, since his unruly mind was determined to stray back to those moments in the
carriage rather than concentrating upon the matters
at hand.

Claredon shifted uneasily on the hard wooden
chair. Good God, now was not the time to be thinking of skin like the richest silk or lips that could
tempt a saint to sin.

Unfortunately, his wayward body still shimmered
with a wicked heat, and that ball of frustration in the
pit of his stomach had hardened to a near unbearable pain.

He did not want to be chasing mysterious
strangers in this crowded, damp inn. He wanted to
be at Longmeade with his wife.

The realization sent a vague sense of alarm
through him.

Desiring a mistress had always been a transitory,
fleeting emotion. Desiring the woman who would be
at his side for eternity seemed to smack of a commitment perilously close to love.

Claredon shifted again. Then his thoughts were abruptly distracted as a pretty barmaid appeared at his side.

"Another ale, my lord?" she demanded with a smile that invited far more pleasures than mere ale could provide.

He gave a shake of his head, barely noting her overripe charms. "Thank you, no."

"There's some shepherd's pie that might tempt yer appetite."

"I have all that I need."

"Yer sure?" the maid demanded, leaning until her exposed cleavage was at eye level. "We aim to please at the King's Arms."

Startled, Claredon experienced no more than irritation at the woman's blatant invitation. What he desired could not be found in this common posting inn. "Quite sure."

"If you change yer mind, you have only to call. My name is Peg." With a flirtatious toss of her raven curls, the maid sauntered away.

Claredon did not bother to watch the seductive sway of her hips or her backward glance. His attention had already returned to the crowd spilling in and out of the room.

More long minutes passed before the sight of his coachman standing in the doorway had Claredon on his feet and rapidly making his way across the room. With a frown, he grasped the servant's arm and maneuvered him into an empty parlor. Shutting the door, he regarded the older man with an impatient gaze. "Johnson, I told you to await me beyond the blacksmith."

"Yes, sir." The servant shifted his feet in a nervous manner. "I fear there has been a bit of trouble."

A terror more sharp and utterly painful than he had ever experienced before stabbed through his heart. "Lady Claredon?" he whispered between stiff lips.

"She is well." Johnson was swift to reassure him. "But we were set upon by a ruffian on the way home."

A dark, lethal fury hardened his countenance. "Tell me from the beginning."

The coachman blanched at the sizzle of danger in the air. "Yes . . . um . . . we had just passed the church when I was halted by a large branch in the road. I got down to pull it aside, and when I turned about, I realized that some scoundrel had opened the door to the carriage. I called out, and he took off across the graveyard. I thought it best to get Lady Claredon to safety rather than to chase after the dastard."

With an effort, Claredon sought to clear his fog of fury. As much as he longed to have his fingers about the unknown villain's neck, it was far more important he see and touch Victoria to reassure himself that she was unharmed.

"You did right," he said in clipped tones. "Gather Peter from the stables, and I will meet you at the carriage."

"Yes, sir."

Leaving his servant, Claredon went in search of the innkeep. He would go to his wife, but first he intended to ensure the stranger did not vanish. It took little time to discover the portly innkeep just leaving the kitchens. With a gesture from Claredon, the man hurried to his side.

"Yes, my lord?"

"I must leave for Longmeade at once, but there is five pounds for you if you send word to me the moment Mr. Smith returns."

A gleam of pure greed entered the man's pale blue eyes, assuring Claredon the innkeeper would hand over his own mother if need be for such a handsome reward. "Yes, sir. You shall know at once."

Confident Mr. Smith could not slip easily away, Claredon turned on his heel and left the inn. His carriage was waiting at the door and, with a meaningful glance at Johnson that silently told him to race with all speed, he climbed into the coach.

He had barely settled onto the seat when they were off. In a blur of passing landscape they traveled the short distance to Longmeade.

Not bothering to wait for the carriage to halt before the sweeping steps, Claredon vaulted out and hurried into the house. The startled butler moved forward with raised brows. "Good afternoon, my lord."

"Where is Lady Claredon?"

"I believe she is in her chambers."

Claredon brushed past the servant and took the stairs two at a time. His burning fear would not be settled until he had seen his wife with his own eyes. Moving down the hall, he came to her door and pushed it open without bothering to knock. Victoria rose from the window seat at his entrance, and he crossed to grasp her hands tightly in his own.

"Victoria, are you harmed?" he rasped in unsteady tones.

"No, I am fine," she assured him with a startled expression.

He briefly closed his eyes as a wave of pure relief rushed through him. "Thank God. I did not think . . . I never should have allowed you to travel without a groom."

Her brows drew together at the edge of self-disgust

in his voice. "Nonsense. You could not know that villain was lying in wait."

Claredon gave a shake of his head, his gut twisting at the mere thought of this beautiful, fragile woman in danger. He would never forgive himself if something were to happen to her. "I should have suspected."

"Nothing happened," she retorted in firm tones. "Beyond giving me a sad fright."

Thrusting aside his anger at having exposed her to danger, Claredon turned his thoughts to the villain. "What occurred?"

"Johnson halted the carriage to remove a branch from the road, and suddenly there was a man at the door pointing a pistol at me."

Claredon's heart came to a full halt. "He was armed?"

"Yes."

"I will kill him," he swore in deadly tones. "What did he want?"

She gave a slow shake of her head. "It was all very odd. He said I possessed his jewels and I was to bring them to the church at midnight tonight."

"Jewels?" he muttered. "What jewels?"

"I haven't the least notion. I have no jewels beyond the pearl necklace that belonged to my mother. No one could possibly believe I had stolen it."

"Bloody hell." Claredon dropped her hands to run his fingers impatiently through his dark hair. "I do not like this."

"I cannot say that I particularly care for it myself," she retorted dryly.

"Did you recognize the man?"

"No. He had a scarf about his lower face and his hat was pulled low upon his brow." She suddenly paused. "Oh."

"What?"

"He had a black cape. Just as the intruder had last night."

Claredon gave a nod of his head. He had already concluded the intruder had been the same dastard who had dared to accost his wife.

What he didn't know was why. Was it a matter of mistaken identity? Had he confused Victoria with some other woman who had his jewels? Or was the man merely mad?

In either case, he intended to put a swift end to this unpleasant business. A very swift end. "Do not worry, my dear. I shall settle this matter."

A hint of concern darkened her eyes. "What will you do?"

"What anyone would do with a rat," he retorted in harsh tones. "I will trap him and then exterminate him."

Seven

Victoria had a very bad feeling in the pit of her stomach.

Pacing across the salon for what seemed to be the hundredth time, she thought of Claredon sitting in the dark graveyard awaiting the appearance of the mysterious Mr. Smith.

She had adamantly argued against his plot to ambush the stranger when he approached the church. What did it matter that he had taken several servants along to surround the area? Or that he had promised not to take foolish chances?

Mr. Smith was obviously a crazed lunatic. If he sensed a trap, there was no telling what might occur.

Reaching the fireplace, Victoria turned on her heel and headed back toward the door. She barely noted the vicar patiently sitting upon the sofa until he heaved a deep sigh.

"My dear Victoria, you are exhausting me," he complained in faintly teasing tones.

Coming to a reluctant halt, Victoria regarded her guest with a rueful grimace. "I cannot seem to help myself, Mr. Humbly," she admitted as she wrapped her arms about her waist. "I never should have allowed Claredon to convince me of this absurd scheme."

The older gentleman lifted his brow at her fierce words. "He did seem rather set upon the notion."

Set upon the notion? He had been positively unrelenting, she thought with a flare of annoyance. "It could be dangerous."

"Surely you desire this scoundrel to be caught?" Humbly demanded.

She gave a restless shrug. The capture of Mr. Smith was not worth her husband's life. "It is the duty of the magistrate. Or if Claredon is truly concerned, we could send to London for a Runner."

"I believe he wished the matter to be settled with all possible speed."

Victoria was not appeased by the argument. "This stranger is clearly deranged. He could be capable of anything."

"All the more reason to capture him swiftly, my dear."

She shook her head. For some reason, the thought of Claredon facing the madman made it difficult to breathe.

"I dislike this waiting. I should have gone with them."

The vicar gave an unexpected laugh. "Good heavens, Lord Claredon never would have agreed to your presence."

Victoria abruptly frowned. She might possess a startlingly fierce concern for Claredon, but she did not bow to his whims. Her independent spirit rebelled at the mere thought. "Lord Claredon may be my husband, but he does not dictate what I may or may not do."

"Oh no, certainly not," Humbly hastily agreed. "I merely meant that there is little either of us could offer tonight. It is far better he has the company of servants who are capable of offering protection."

"I suppose," she reluctantly conceded.

"And besides, Lord Claredon strikes me as a very capable gentleman," he was swift to add. "I am certain he will have the situation well in hand."

"He is not always capable," she corrected, as she recalled his impulsive decision to succumb to the wiles of Lady Westfield. "He can do remarkably foolish things upon occasion."

"Ah." The word held a wealth of meaning, and she blushed as she realized the vicar had easily followed her train of thought. "Tell me, Victoria, do you blame Lord Claredon for forcing the two of you to wed?"

Caught off guard by the abrupt question, Victoria felt her blush deepen. "I . . . in some ways, I suppose," she stammered, unable to baldly lie beneath that piercing gaze.

"Even though it was all nothing more than a rather unfortunate misunderstanding?" he charged.

Misunderstanding? Victoria blinked in shock, wondering if Humbly had forgotten the precise events leading to her scandalous marriage.

"Rather more than a misunderstanding," she felt compelled to point out. "He bribed a maid to unlock my door and slipped into my bed."

"Not precisely your bed," he corrected in firm tones.

Victoria could not help but be rather shocked at his seeming nonchalance toward her husband's rakish habits. "He should not have entered any lady's bedchamber."

"True enough," he conceded with a faint smile. "But in his defense, he did believe he would be welcomed.

Had you not attempted to hide your own identity, he never would have troubled you."

It was a realization that Victoria preferred to forget. After all, she had meant no harm by her small deceit. And if not for Claredon, no one would have ever discovered the truth.

"I hardly could have used my own name," she said defensively.

His gaze was speculative. "No, I do not suppose you could have."

Discomforted by that gaze, she gave a small shrug. "Besides, I could not have suspected that pretending to be Lady Westfield would create such a disaster."

"I have often discovered the simplest deceits can lead to disaster."

Victoria stiffened in disbelief. She had thought this gentleman her friend. Should he not be offering her comfort rather than condemnation? "Do you mean to imply that you consider me at fault for what occurred?"

He gave a helpless lift of his hand. "I just wonder if perhaps both of you possess a measure of blame."

The urge to deny any share of the blame was halted upon her lips. As difficult as it might be to face, she did know deep within her that if she had not set aside her common sense and decided to elope with Thomas, she never would have been at that particular inn, nor would she have used her cousin's name.

Just as importantly, she was belatedly aware she had forgotten her determination to assure Mr. Humbly that she was quite satisfied with her marriage. Her wits were clearly more rattled than she had suspected by the appearance of the stranger and Claredon's determination to capture him. "It does not matter now. It is over and done with," she said in determinedly offhand tones.

His sherry eyes narrowed. "Not if you harbor a lingering resentment toward your own husband."

With an awkward motion, Victoria turned to pace back toward the fireplace, effectively hiding her expression. His words were far too close for comfort. "Of course I do not. I have told you, it is all in the past. We have reconciled ourselves to the marriage."

There was a short pause before Humbly cleared his throat. "That is for the best. God often works in mysterious ways and the paths he leads us to are not always of our own choosing. But in the end, I believe it is usually for the best."

Victoria's lips twisted. She did not believe God had any hand in the less than honorable reasons she and Claredon had ended up in the same posting inn. Still, if it comforted Humbly to believe her marriage was God's will, who was she to disillusion him? "Yes," she murmured.

"And Lord Claredon will make you a fine husband, Victoria," he continued, unaware of her unease. "Although I have only spoken with him briefly, I am convinced he is determined to be a good and faithful husband to you."

His words closely echoed Claredon's, sending a poignant ache through her.

Her body was already far too vulnerable to the maddening magic her husband could weave. Did she desire her heart and soul to be vulnerable as well? A shiver shook her body as she shied from the dangerous question.

Now was not the time to be considering such bothersome emotions, she told herself as she turned back to face the vicar. Her thoughts should be firmly focused on ensuring Claredon returned home safely.

After that . . . well, it was a worry for another day.

"I believe Claredon is more determined to get himself killed than to be a good husband," she said in impatient tones. "Where are they? It is well past midnight."

Offering a sympathetic smile, Humbly gave a lift of his hands.

"It could be that the mysterious gentleman has not yet arrived."

Victoria gnawed her bottom lip, unable to halt herself from considering all the numerous disasters that might have occurred. "Or that he did not come alone and Claredon is in danger."

"We must not think the worst," Humbly chastised gently.

"Perhaps we should go and ascertain that nothing has gone amiss," she abruptly suggested.

Not surprisingly, Humbly gave a firm shake of his head. "Good heavens, Lord Claredon would have my head upon a platter if I so much as allowed you to step foot outside this house. Have mercy upon me, my dear."

She twisted her hands together, detesting the feeling of being utterly helpless. She was a woman accustomed to taking command, not waiting about like some vaporish miss. "But if he is in trouble . . ."

"He has two grooms and Johnson with him," Humbly interrupted in tones that defied argument. "If there has been trouble, one of them would have returned to warn us."

"If they were able," she said in pointed tones.

"You are allowing your imagination to overrule your common sense, Victoria."

Her features hardened with determination. "I still maintain we should go and ascertain that nothing has occurred."

"Absolutely not," the vicar retorted, rising to his feet as if he would physically restrain her if necessary.

"Mr. Humbly," she began, placing her hands upon her hips. Her commanding words, however, were abruptly interrupted by the sound of footsteps in the foyer. Sharp relief raced through her. "They have returned."

Not bothering to wait for Mr. Humbly, Victoria raced from the room and down the stairs. From there it was only a short distance to the foyer, where she was brought to a startled halt at the sight of her husband being held upright by the two burly grooms. Her heart stuttered to a halt as her horrified gaze took in his disheveled appearance and the unmistakable darkness of blood staining the shoulder of his coat. "Dear God, Claredon, you are injured," she breathed.

Abruptly turning his head to discover her standing in the shadows, Claredon forced a rueful smile to his lips. "Just a trifling scratch, I assure you."

"Trifling?" she stepped into the pool of light offered by the gilded chandelier. "You are bleeding."

"The demon took a shot at us, my lady," one of the grooms explained. "I told his lordship to stay down, but he would have to charge after him."

Victoria felt a flood of fury rush through her at the knowledge Claredon had so ridiculously endangered his life. Blast it all, did the man not possess the smallest grain of sense? "You charged after an armed criminal?" she demanded, her eyes smoldering with a dangerous fire.

"Did you wish him to slip away so he could remain a danger to you?" he countered in grim tones.

She was furiously unimpressed with his attempt at logic. "I did not desire you to take such foolish chances. You could have been killed."

"Highly unlikely," he denied. "The scoundrel was too busy attempting to flee to take proper aim. It was only the devil's own luck he managed to clip me."

Her stomach twisted in pain at his careless words. A few more inches and the bullet would have been in his heart. The thought was unbearable. He had no right to take such absurd risks with his life.

No right at all.

Glancing toward the door, where the coachman cowardly attempted to avoid her restrained anger, she stabbed him with a steely frown. "Johnson, go for the doctor," she commanded in clipped tones. "You two take Lord Claredon up to his bed. I shall be up in a moment."

"Victoria, there is no need for a doctor," Claredon protested. "It is nothing more than a flesh wound."

The near patronizing tone in his voice abruptly snapped her composure.

First being forced to wait at home while he played cat and mouse with the dangerous villain and now being treated like an overanxious nitwit was enough to infuriate the most patient of women. "You listen to me," she gritted, pointing a finger directly in his face. "I am furious and not at all in humor to listen to your vain displays of ridiculous courage. A doctor will be fetched, you will go to bed, and I will be up to clean the wound in a moment. Is that clear?"

There was a shocked silence before Claredon's lips suddenly twitched with suppressed amusement. "Astonishingly clear, my dove," he murmured in meek tones.

Victoria gave a satisfied sniff. "Good."

* * *

Claredon was accustomed to being fussed over. With a mother and seven older sisters, he had not been able to skin his knee without a clutch of women tending to him with tender concern.

But he discovered it startlingly delightful to have his wife hovering over him as the doctor stitched together the crease made by the errant bullet. Almost as delightful as her tucking the blankets about him as the older gentleman packed his belongings and left the room.

Despite her grim expression, she could not entirely hide the concern smoldering deep in her eyes. The knowledge stirred an odd tenderness in his heart. However cold she pretended to be, she did care in some small measure.

He breathed in her warm, sweet scent as she arranged the pillows behind him. Ah yes, this was indeed more pleasant than the fussing of his mother and sisters, he acknowledged with a new stirring that had nothing to do with his heart.

With a small tug, he could have her on the bed beside him, he thought with a flare of anticipation. And he could forget all about the aggravating hours he had spent crouching in the dark, only to have the scoundrel sense the waiting trap and slip away.

She slowly straightened, bringing an end to any hope she might accidentally topple forward into his arms, and Claredon heaved a faint sigh.

It seemed he would have yet another night alone in his wide, empty bed.

Settling against the pillows, he regarded her with a faint smile. "I did tell you that it was no more than a flesh wound."

Her lips thinned with a simmering disapproval. "The most simple wound can kill if it is not properly attended to."

"Yes, my dear," he murmured, his lips twitching. "Are you determined to remain angry forever?"

"You took a ridiculous risk."

"I do not want this villain running about the neighborhood," he said in stern tones.

"It is the duty of the magistrate to capture him."

"It is my duty to keep you safe." He reached out to grasp her hand, his thumb gently rubbing her cold fingers. "I will not rest until the madman is locked away or dead."

"I . . ." She appeared lost for words as a delightful blush warmed her cheeks.

The hint of vulnerability in his staunchly independent wife was rather wonderful, Claredon decided. It gave him hope that she might have need of him, even if she was not yet prepared to admit it. "Does it surprise you to know that I am determined to protect my wife?" he asked softly.

She gave a flustered shrug. "I am unaccustomed to having anyone concern themselves with my protection."

"Then it is high time someone did so." Keeping her gaze locked with his own, he lifted her hand to press a kiss upon her palm. He felt a satisfying tremor race through her. "And in truth, it is a pleasure to be your champion."

Just for a moment there was a glimpse of deep longing in her beautiful eyes, a poignant ache to love and be loved. But just as he touched his lips to the frantic pulse of her inner wrist, she abruptly pulled away and resumed her role as the chastising wife.

"You will not be my champion for long if you continue to take ridiculous risks with your life."

Claredon squashed his flare of impatience with her instinctive retreat. The one thing he had discovered in the past few months was that Victoria could not be rushed. To try and demand more than she was willing to give would only push her further away.

"How fierce you sound, my dear," he said in deliberately light tones.

She placed her hands upon her hips. "I am attempting to make you be reasonable."

His gaze slowly lowered over her slender body, which was temptingly outlined by the soft muslin gown.

"Ah, but a husband is not meant to be reasonable when defending his wife. He is meant to be fearless."

She gave a click of her tongue. "Will you please be serious?"

"I am serious." His gaze lifted to lock within her own, his expression hardening with determination. The knowledge that some strange man had dared to halt his wife's carriage and to point a gun at her burned like a fever in the pit of his stomach. He would make the man pay for his audacity, no matter what it took. "Deadly serious. The villain escaped tonight, but he will not be so fortunate on the next occasion."

Clearly sensing the cold intent in his voice, Victoria frowned in concern. "What do you intend to do?"

He gave a lift of his uninjured shoulder. "I already have servants watching the grounds, and the innkeep has promised to send word the moment Mr. Smith returns to his room. It will not be long before I have him cornered."

She took an impulsive step forward, her hands

clenched together. "Promise me you will not approach him again without the magistrate."

He gave a slow shake of his head. "I cannot do that, Victoria."

Without warning, she seated herself on the edge of the bed and grasped his hands in a tight grip. "I want your promise," she commanded.

A flare of pure heat raced through him as her hip pressed against his thigh. He had devoted too many long nights to imagining her laid upon this bed, her fiery curls spread across the pillow and her slender limbs wrapped about him, to remain immune to her proximity.

All his noble intentions to be patient and undemanding were suddenly strained to the very limit by a rush of fierce desire. "Do you know, I quite like this side of you, dearest," he murmured softly.

She dropped his hands as if she had been scalded, her expression suddenly wary. "What?"

He smiled as he trailed his fingers up the length of her arm. Tracing her shoulder, then the provocative bare skin of her neck, he at last sought the satin fire of her hair and began removing the offending clips that held it in a tidy knot. "All this fussing and concern over my welfare is quite bewitching."

Her eyes darkened as the curls spilled about her shoulders. "Claredon," she breathed.

"Yes, my dear?" he murmured, running his fingers through her glorious hair.

"I . . . what are you doing?"

He smoothed the hair over her shoulder, then daringly allowed his questing fingers to follow the neckline of her gown. "Making you more comfortable," he said in husky tones, his lower body clenching with need as his fingers lightly brushed the swell of her breast.

She swallowed heavily, her breath coming in shallow gasps. "You are ill. You should not be moving about."

Claredon did not feel ill. In truth, he had never felt more gloriously alive than he did at this moment. Every sense had been heightened until his entire body tingled with awareness of the woman seated so close to him—the warm scent of her skin, the luscious softness of her breast beneath his fingers, and the press of her hip against the hardness of his thigh.

It was enough to send him up in flames.

"I have told you it is no more than a scratch," he assured her, rather surprised when his voice came out in a low rasp.

"Still, you need your rest."

He gave a low chuckle. "I would prefer a kiss."

"Claredon," she breathed, attempting to appear scandalized, but only managing to be endearingly bewildered.

"I did risk my life for you, Victoria," he teased. "Surely I deserve some sort of reward?"

"You deserve a good hiding for your foolishness," she retorted, but her voice had lost its sting.

"Be kind, my wife," he whispered, desperately willing her to give freely of herself. "I will not rest until I have received a small token from you."

There was a long, tense silence before she slowly leaned forward. Claredon's breath caught as her lips softly brushed over his own.

Swift, shimmering pleasure flooded through him. He groaned as his hand gently cupped her breast, his skin tingling as her hair caressed the bare skin of his chest. Never, never had he wanted a woman with such a blazing intensity, to bury himself deep within her sweet innocence and forget the world.

And yet he made no move to halt her as she slowly pulled away.

Suddenly he realized why he had urged himself to wait, why he did not want to seduce his wife against her will and against her heart: He wanted her to give of herself unconditionally.

Perhaps baffled at his restraint, Victoria rose to her feet and nervously ran her hands over the folds of her skirt. "I will leave you now. If you have need of anything, you have only to call."

"Thank you, my dear."

"Yes, well . . . good night."

He folded his hands over his stomach as she edged toward the door. Soon, he assured his renegade body. Soon she would belong to him heart, soul and body.

He could accept no less.

Eight

The sketch was not going particularly well.

The arrangement of flowers that the gardener had gathered for her upon the wrought iron table in the conservatory was certainly lovely enough. Roses, daffodils, and rare Holland tulips offered a vivid splash of color in the slanting morning sunlight, but at last Victoria had to concede that her heart simply was not upon her drawing this fine morning.

As was becoming all too familiar, her thoughts seemed determined to dwell upon the gentleman who was responsible for yet another sleepless night.

She was still furious that he had dared to behave in such a reckless fashion. To even think of him charging through the dark in pursuit of an armed lunatic made her blood run cold. And the knowledge that he could so easily dismiss a bullet wound that might have been fatal—but for the grace of God—left a knot of unease in the pit of her stomach.

Last night she had been torn between the desire to shake some sense into his thick skull and to hold him and never let him go. She had wanted to punish him for daring to be such a fool and yet, deep within her, she had longed to reassure herself he was safe and well.

It was a frightening realization.

The very fact that she had reacted with such violent emotions to the horror he had been injured revealed that she was not nearly as indifferent to her husband as she had believed. And that brief, searing kiss had only confirmed her fears.

She closed her eyes and breathed in deeply.

For months she had done her best to avoid Claredon. By keeping a reasonable distance from him, she thought to keep herself protected from his potent charm. But now she could no longer deny that it did not matter if he were next to her or miles away. He invaded her thoughts with a persistence that was utterly unnerving.

"Good morning, my dear." A softly masculine voice broke into her dark imaginings.

Wrenching her eyes open, Victoria turned her head to discover Claredon surveying her with a probing gaze.

Uneasily, she wondered how long he had been watching her, and, more importantly, just how much of her inner uncertainty had been revealed upon her face. It was unnerving to think he had sensed just how desperately vulnerable she was beneath her staunch air of invincibility. "Claredon, what are you doing out of bed?" she demanded in tones more sharp than she had intended.

His blue eyes narrowed as he stepped forward. Attired in a bottle green coat and silver waistcoat, he appeared undeservingly healthy and altogether too handsome for any maiden's peace of mind.

"I am not an invalid, Victoria," he retorted in a determinedly mild voice. "My shoulder is a bit stiff, nothing more."

She drew in a deep breath to calm her edgy nerves. "You must still take care not to reopen the wound."

"I wished to speak with you."

"Then you should have sent a servant to find me," she retorted, feeling far safer in the role of scolding wife than uncertain maiden. "I would have come to you."

As if sensing her determined chastisement was hiding her vivid awareness of his masculine presence, his lips curved in a rather wicked smile. "The notion certainly entered my mind, but I thought it wiser to resist temptation."

Her expression became wary. "I would not have minded."

With slow, deliberate movements, he crossed the small distance until he was close enough to stroke a hand down her cheek. "I fear my . . . restraint would have not withstood another visit to my bedchamber, Victoria," he said in husky tones. "I want you very much, and having you seated next to me upon my bed gives rise to all sorts of wicked desires."

She shivered as his simmering blue gaze stroked warmly over her upturned countenance.

"Oh," she murmured, briefly lost in the sensuous pleasure of his fingers, which softly moved to trace the curve of her lips. She had dreamed of those fingers last night, the feel of them tracing patterns of delicious heat over her skin and stirring smoldering passions to life that she only dimly understood.

The realization that those passions were indeed being stirred, and not just in her dreams, brought Victoria to her feet with a jerky motion. Dear heavens, she would soon be swooning whenever he entered the room.

A most humiliating prospect.

On the point of fleeing, Victoria was halted as

Claredon abruptly reached out to grasp her hand in a firm grip.

"Wait, my dear, there is no need to bolt," he said with soft insistence. "I did not come here this morning to seduce you. I am determined to wait until you are prepared to come to me of your own will."

She slowly turned to face him, unconsciously wetting her oddly dry lips. She did not particularly care for the thought he was merely biding his time until she caved in to temptation.

"And what if I never do?" she challenged.

He shrugged, supremely indifferent to the threat. "Then I have only myself to blame."

Somehow his unwavering belief that his seduction of her was inevitable sent an arrow of fear straight to the center of her being. It should be ridiculous. Such confidence in his abilities only revealed his utter arrogance. But with her skin still tingling from his touch and her body weary from her restless night, she was not nearly as self-assured as she would like to be.

Determinedly, she pulled her arm free of his grasp and sought to pretend an indifference she was far from feeling. "What did you wish to speak with me about?"

His lips twisted, as if battling his instinctive urge to rattle her fragile composure, but thankfully he turned the conversation to his reason for seeking her out.

"I would like your promise that you will not leave Longmeade without me."

She blinked in surprise. "What?"

"Just until this madman is captured," he explained in firm tones.

"But surely I would be safe enough with a footman with me?"

His expression became somber as his eyes darkened with determination. "We cannot be certain how far this scoundrel is prepared to go, Victoria. You would not wish to put the lives of our servants in danger, would you?"

She knew without a doubt that he was only using her concern for the staff to force her to obey his command. The villain had shown no desire to put anyone but herself and Claredon at risk. But while she could be stubborn, perhaps at times even overly proud, she was at heart sensible. She had no desire to encounter the dangerous Mr. Smith, nor to lead any of her servants into his unpredictable path.

"No, of course not," she agreed.

He grimaced at the edge in her voice. "It will be for only a few days. And you will have Mr. Humbly for company."

She gave a restless shake of her head. "I do not like this."

Claredon abruptly moved forward to cup her chin in gentle fingers. "I am not attempting to steal your independence from you," he said gently, misunderstanding her sudden flare of annoyance. "I merely wish you to realize the danger."

"It is not that," she retorted with a frustrated sigh. "It is annoying this Mr. Smith is allowed to disrupt our lives in such a manner."

Almost absently his fingers trailed up the line of her jaw. "Yes, he has a great deal to answer for. Do not doubt that I will see him punished."

Sharp pleasure surged through her, but Victoria refused to be distracted. She was sensible enough to recognize the danger, but she was not nearly so certain Claredon could be convinced to behave in a reasonable manner.

"And what of you?" she demanded.

His gaze followed the path of his fingers as they lightly moved over her cheek. "What do you mean?"

"I wish your promise not to take any further risks."

His lips curved as he captured a stray curl and wrapped it about his finger. "I assure you, I will be on guard at all times. I have no intention of allowing the villain another shot at me."

Her brows drew together at his evasive answer. "You are not to be going out alone."

His brows rose at the stern expression upon her countenance. "Is that a command?" he murmured softly.

"It is a request to use your common sense," she countered in tones that warned him she would not be thwarted on this.

He regarded her for a long moment before a slow smile shimmered in his blue eyes. "I suppose it is only fair that I have the same stipulations upon my movements as you," he softly conceded. "Shall we seal our promises with a kiss?"

Now that she had been assured he would not be out hunting the lunatic on his own, Victoria suddenly became aware of just how close Claredon had moved. Shimmering heat lay like a thick cloak about her, clouding her mind and urging her to lower the barriers between them. It did not help that those distracting fingers continued to stroke the soft skin of her temple or that his gaze had lowered to rest upon her lips. With unnerving ease, he had managed to stir those tempting sensations that she had battled to subdue throughout the long night.

"I do not think that will be necessary," she said in an oddly thick voice.

He lowered his head to breathe in deeply of the

scent of her freshly washed hair. "Perhaps not precisely necessary, but certainly enjoyable."

"Claredon."

His hand cupped her cheek, tilting her head until she was a mere breath from his lips. "Yes, my dear?"

"I thought . . . you said . . ."

"I said that I would wait to make you my wife until you are ready to come to me," he murmured, lightly brushing his lips over her own. "That does not mean we cannot enjoy a harmless kiss."

Slowly his lips teased over her mouth, featherlight and lingering only long enough to create an ache of need deep within her. She wanted to put her arms about his neck and force those lips to kiss her properly, to lean forward so that her body was arched against the warm power of his own. Her hands even fluttered to the solid strength of his wide chest before the door to the conservatory was suddenly pushed open and the fragile bewitchment was shattered.

Abruptly Victoria pulled away from her husband, fiercely telling herself that she was relieved by the timely interruption, even if her body did tremble in protest at the sudden end to the pleasurable caresses.

The clearly embarrassed footman cleared his throat as his face flushed with heat. "Pardon me, my lord."

More annoyed than ashamed at having been discovered making love to his wife in the middle of the conservatory, Claredon placed his hands upon his hips and glared at the poor servant. "What is it?"

The footman shifted uneasily beneath the obvious irritation of his employer. "There is a gentleman here to see Lady Claredon," he stammered.

"A gentleman?" Claredon demanded in surprise.

"Yes, sir. A Mr. Stice."

Victoria took a startled step forward. "Thomas?"

A dangerous stillness settled about Claredon as he slowly turned to stab her with a glittering gaze. "What is he doing here?"

"I haven't the faintest notion," she retorted with genuine confusion.

She had not spoken with Thomas since the morning he had belatedly arrived at the posting inn to discover that she and Claredon had hastily announced they were engaged and soon to be wed. Not surprisingly, the poor man had been thoroughly baffled and more than a little hurt. He had barely listened to Victoria's stammered confession of the horrid scene that she had endured the evening before, clearly wanting to be far away from the scandal swirling about her.

Staunchly, Victoria had told herself that it was only natural that Thomas would desire to avoid the ugly rumors. Such a sensitive young gentleman could not be expected to readily expose himself to that sort of embarrassment. And he had been thinking only of her when he kept silent about their botched elopement. After all, to admit the truth would only add fuel to the malicious gossip.

But, perhaps selfishly, she could not wholly deny a bit of disappointment that he had so easily walked away from her. Not once had he tried to contact her. And certainly he had made no effort to save her from Claredon by offering to wed her himself. When it came to the sticking point, it had been a scandalous rake who had saved her reputation rather than the gentleman who claimed to love her.

A scandalous rake who was currently regarding

her with a dark frown. "Mr. Stice did not write to tell you he was coming?" he demanded.

Victoria gave a shake of her head. "No."

Without allowing his narrowed gaze to stray from her pale face, Claredon waved a dismissive hand toward the waiting servant. In obvious relief, he readily slipped out of the conservatory and softly closed the door behind him.

Victoria discovered herself uneasily clasping her hands together. Her husband was no longer the teasing seducer of mere moments ago. Instead, there was a distinctly predatory cast to his features and a dangerous glitter in his eyes. "I do not want you seeing Mr. Stice," he said in clipped tones.

The preemptory command instantly rasped against Victoria's pride. She would not be intimidated nor bullied by any man, especially her husband. "Do not be absurd, Claredon," she retorted with a lift of her chin. "I must discover why he is here. It might very well be important."

"Then I will speak with him."

"He came to see me."

"Only because he is a fool. If he possessed the least amount of sense, he would have realized his danger."

She frowned at his incomprehensible words, not at all liking his sudden attempt to intimidate her. "Are you forbidding me to see Thomas?" she demanded in a tight voice.

His features hardened as he realized her own growing irritation. No doubt he had expected her to simply concede to his unreasonable demands. "Why would you wish to see him?" he rasped. "I am your husband now, whether you like it or not."

"Well I certainly do not like it at the moment," she

charged back, an annoyed flush darkening her cheeks. "You are treating me like a child."

He moved until he was towering over her, refusing to back down from his stubborn stance. "No, I am treating you as my wife. I do not wish you to be with the gentleman you were once determined to wed. Surely that is reasonable?"

"It is ludicrous. What do you suppose could occur in our front parlor?"

A humorless smile curled his lips. "Shall I go into detail?"

Victoria's blush abruptly deepened as she slowly comprehended his implication.

The rat.

She did not doubt that he was quite an expert at seducing married women in their own front parlor. Or anywhere else, for that matter.

"I suppose you would know," she said in cold tones. "However, you need have no fear that I shall allow Thomas to ravish me beneath my husband's roof. I do have my standards."

He did not even possess the grace to flush at her sharp barb. Instead he stabbed her with a steely gaze. "And why should I trust you, Victoria?" he growled. "You possess no faith in me."

She flinched at the direct accusation. She could hardly deny her lack of faith. It was the reason she consistently kept a wall of restraint between them and why she did not succumb to his practiced seduction.

Oddly, however, she found she did not particularly care to have her own honor questioned. She suddenly realized just how impossible it was to defend such an intangible quality.

"I will not be dictated to, Claredon," she instead

retorted, her expression set in stubborn lines. "You are my husband, not my master. Now, if you will excuse me, I have a guest awaiting me."

"Victoria . . ."

She easily sidestepped the hand he reached out to capture her with and headed directly for the door. She was not about to be lectured to by Claredon, nor told what she could or could not do. Fate might have forced her into marriage with the man, but that did not mean she had to become one of those spineless wives who bowed to their husband's every whim.

With her head held high, she swept from the conservatory and moved directly toward the front parlor. She almost half expected to hear Claredon charging behind her, but thankfully he appeared to have conceded defeat.

She unconsciously slowed her steps, feeling the most ridiculous pang of guilt. It was not that she regretted her determination to battle his arrogant commands. She possessed far too much pride to be browbeaten into submission. But a renegade part of her could not help but rue the knowledge that their temporary truce seemed to be at an end. Once again they were enemies, with nothing in common but their animosity.

It was a disheartening realization.

Attempting to push aside her unwelcome thoughts, Victoria entered the front parlor and forced a smile to her lips as the young, slender gentleman with pale brown hair hurriedly rose to his feet. "Thomas, what a surprise," she murmured as she moved forward and allowed him to grasp her hands in a tight grip.

"Oh, Victoria, it is so good to see you," he breathed, his youthful features set in lines of relief.

Expecting a sharp pang at being in the company of the gentleman she had once loved, Victoria was surprised to discover she felt no more than a vague fondness at the sight of his familiar countenance. "Will you have a seat?"

Waiting until she had settled upon the sofa, Thomas returned to his chair and regarded her with a rather wistful smile. "You look as beautiful as ever, Victoria."

"Thank you."

"Are you . . . happy?"

Victoria stiffened, not at all eager to discuss her marriage with this man. He had not seemed to care about her happiness when she had been caught in the scandal. It was rather late to consider her feelings at this date. "As happy as could be expected," she hedged.

"That is good," he said in vague tones, almost as if he had not even heard her words.

Realizing that Thomas clearly had not come to reassure himself that she was well taken care of by Claredon, she smiled wryly. It probably had not entered his thoughts to concern himself with her well being once she had been handed over to her husband. "And how are you?"

He heaved a tragic sigh. "Miserable."

"Your mother?" she inquired, all too aware of Mrs. Stice's habit of bullying her only son.

"Yes. She is demanding that I wed Miss Calloway."

Victoria swallowed a resigned sigh. It had been his mother's determination to wed him to a fortune that had led to their aborted elopement. At the time, she had been convinced that the only means of saving poor Thomas was to wed in secret. Now she felt more than a hint of impatience at the realization he was still at the mercy of Mrs. Stice's overbearing habits.

Had he learned nothing from his brief attempt at independence?

"She cannot force you to do anything against your will," she said with a faint frown. "You are of an age to make your own decisions."

A petulant expression marred his soft features. "You know how she can be. She has been making my life miserable since our attempted elopement. I cannot walk out the door without a servant telling her where I have gone and with whom I have spoken. She is determined to keep me from forming an attachment to another woman."

"Have you considered setting up your own establishment?"

"It is what I would like above all things, but Mother would never allow me to leave her."

Not quite certain what Thomas expected her to do about his mother's interference, she gave a sigh. Surely he could not believe that he could still depend upon her to save him now that she was wed to Lord Claredon? It was one thing to expect her help when they were secretly engaged. It was quite another when her loyalty now lay with her husband.

Still, Thomas could be remarkably impervious to others when he chose. And it was quite possible that he had not even considered the notion it was highly improper to seek out the company of his former fiancée or to realize she might be offended by the knowledge he had sought her out only to request her help.

"What brings you to Longmeade?" she demanded in resigned tones.

He gave a discomforted cough. "Well . . . I fear that I had a rather heated squabble with Mother when she accused me of stealing her jewels."

Victoria blinked in sudden surprise. Jewels? What an extraordinarily odd coincidence that his mother would be missing her jewels just when there was a crazed lunatic accusing her of possessing his jewels. "What?"

"It is all no more than a mare's nest," Thomas complained. "She no doubt left them in Derbyshire or had them sent out to be cleaned."

"How very odd."

"Not really. She will use any excuse to believe I am attempting to sneak away from her. As if I would pawn her jewels for my own pleasure."

"Yes."

At last sensing her distraction, Thomas leaned forward with a frown. "What is it, Victoria?"

She gave a sharp shake of her head. Mrs. Stice and her jewels had nothing to do with the mysterious Mr. Smith. "Nothing," she retorted in firm tones. "You still have not told me what you are doing in Kent."

A hint of color washed over the pale countenance. "I fear I became so angered by my mother's accusations I simply stormed from the house and swore I would never return."

Decidedly surprised by the younger man's rare display of courage, Victoria regarded him in amazement. "Good heavens."

He shifted uneasily in his chair. "Unfortunately, I had no notion of where to go. Then, I thought of you and . . . well, here I am."

"I see," she said slowly.

"Would it be a terrible imposition if I were to stay here a few days?" he pleaded, clearly not at all aware of the unseemliness of his request. Or the danger of facing Claredon. "Just until I have proven to Mother that she cannot speak to me in such a manner?"

Victoria shivered at the mere thought of her husband's reaction to having Thomas as a houseguest. For goodness sakes, he had been thoroughly unreasonable at having her speak with her former fiancé at all. He was bound to be furious at her request to allow Thomas to remain for an indefinite stay.

"Well . . ."

"I promise not to be any bother," Thomas softly coaxed.

Victoria gnawed her bottom lip, torn between her reluctance to press Claredon into enduring the company of a gentleman he openly disliked, and poor Thomas's pleading request.

It was at last her own inability to turn away a person in need that swayed her decision. Longmeade was as much her home as Claredon's now, she staunchly told herself. And despite all that had occurred, Thomas was still her friend. It would be unconscionable to turn him away when he was so obviously distressed.

Still, she could not deny a distinct chill of unease as she gave a slow nod of her head. "Of course."

Thomas clapped his hands together in relief. "I knew I could depend upon you, Victoria. You have always been my greatest friend."

Wishing that he had chosen another friend to depend upon, Victoria rose to her feet. She would have to find Claredon and admit she had offered sanctuary to Thomas before he could learn the truth from the servants.

"I will have a room prepared for you," she murmured.

Thomas rose to his feet. "And you will not allow Mother to know I am here?"

She resisted the urge to roll her eyes at his anxious

tone. The gentleman could not help his weak nature, any more than she could help her habit of commanding others. "I have no intention of contacting your mother," she assured him in dry tones.

"Thank you," he breathed.

Victoria gave a wry smile as she walked out of the door.

In the first weeks of her marriage, she had often thought of Thomas, foolishly hoping he would suddenly appear to whisk her away from the mess she had made of her life. Even with her disappointment in his lack of determination to make her his bride whatever the scandal, she had thought anything would be preferable to being tied to Claredon for all eternity.

It was rather ironic that now he had appeared, she realized that his presence would never have solved her troubles. Not only did he not possess the strength to fight for her, but he was far too enwrapped in his own needs to consider her own.

Utterly unlike Claredon, she grudgingly conceded.

Had the woman he had chosen to marry been forced to wed another, he never would have meekly stood aside. Instead he would have battled to the death to keep her at his side—a knowledge that made her heart twitch with a sudden ache of loss.

She had loyally attempted to maintain her shining image of her love for Thomas. She wanted to believe that it had been utterly pure and right. Having seen him today, she very much feared that glowing memory was in danger of being tarnished.

The notion made her heart decidedly uneasy. That lingering belief, that she still loved Thomas, had been a potent weapon in fighting off Claredon's charm.

And she very much feared she needed all the weapons she could muster.

Nine

Despite the early hour, Claredon swallowed a large gulp of brandy. He had handled Victoria badly.

A wry smile touched his grim countenance. Bloody hell, he always handled Victoria badly. For a man reputed to be a master with the fairer sex, he was remarkably incompetent when it came to his own wife. But this morning he had been particularly clumsy.

The moment he had learned of Mr. Stice's arrival, he had lost all sense. A fury had whipped through him as incomprehensible as it was unstoppable.

How dare the cowardly fool show his face at Longmeade?

It was bad enough that Stice maintained a place in his wife's heart. To actually dare to thrust his way back into her life went beyond the pale. He wanted to rush to the front parlor and physically toss the man from his home. Or, better yet, run him off with a horsewhip for even daring to trespass upon his land.

Only the knowledge that Victoria would never forgive him for treating her precious Thomas in such a fashion kept him pacing the library rather than relieving the tension knotted in the pit of his stomach.

Damn it all.

Why could she not see that the gentleman was utterly unworthy of her loyalty? He had done nothing to save her when she had been embroiled in scandal. He had not once offered his assistance or even his regret that their marriage was not to be. Instead he had fled like a frightened milksop with no thought for his trapped fiancée. Emotions perilously close to jealousy battered his mind as he paced through the library, until a new, startling thought abruptly swept aside his unwelcome broodings.

Coming to a halt, he allowed himself to ponder the sudden suspicion that bloomed to life, not even noticing that the door to the library had been softly opened and that a short, rotund gentleman was silently regarding him with a shrewd gaze.

"Good morning, my lord." Mr. Humbly interrupted his musings.

Abruptly turning about, Claredon regarded the vicar with an impatient gaze. "Humbly."

"I trust you are feeling better?"

Claredon grimaced, realizing he could hardly disguise his black mood. "I was."

As always, the vicar maintained his air of placid goodwill. Claredon wondered if anything beyond a thief slipping into the window could manage to rattle the older man. "Has something occurred?"

"Mr. Stice has come for a visit."

"Mr. Stice?" Humbly furrowed his brow. "Why is that name familiar?"

"He is the gentleman with whom Victoria attempted to elope."

Comprehension dawned as Humbly gave a slow nod of his head. "Ah."

"She, of course, insisted upon seeing him."

Humbly tilted his head to one side and regarded him in a curious fashion. "You did not wish her to?"

That dark, unpleasant sensation twisted his gut once again. "No."

"Why?"

Claredon's features hardened at the vicar's probing. Really, the man could not be that unworldly, he seethed. "I think it would be obvious," he said in tight tones. "Victoria believes herself to be in love with the man."

Humbly frowned with obvious disapproval at his words. "Victoria will not forget that she is now wed to you," he said in chastising tones.

Claredon polished off the last of the brandy before setting his glass on the nearby desk with restrained violence. "I do not fear her being unfaithful," he retorted.

Humbly slowly moved forward, his gaze watchful. "Then what do you fear?"

"That she will recall why she desired to wed him rather than me." There was a stark silence as he grudgingly revealed the betraying emotions that twisted his gut. It was not easy to speak the words out loud. He did, after all, have his pride, and it was not pleasant to accept that his own wife obviously preferred another man. Or that the knowledge gnawed at him in a manner he was not utterly comfortable in examining.

Thankfully Humbly did not smirk at how low he had fallen, nor attempt to pass off his worries with a flippant response. Instead he seemed to consider his response for a long moment.

"I certainly am not an expert when it comes to women," he admitted with a kindly smile. "But I think it is far more likely that Victoria will begin to realize that marriage with Mr. Stice would have been a grave mistake."

Claredon frowned at the tempting words. "But she believes she is in love with him."

"Oh, she certainly convinced herself that she loved him," Humbly readily agreed. "But during our discussions, I have noted that she spoke far more of her effort to save him from his overbearing mother than of her emotional attachment to him. Victoria has always been a woman who rushed to the rescue of others."

Although the vicar's words closely reflected his own belief in Victoria's affection for the hapless Mr. Stice, it offered little comfort at the moment. "I agree that marriage would have been a disaster between Victoria and the bumbling nitwit, but it is impossible to convince my wife of the truth. Believe me, I have tried."

"Then perhaps it is best to allow her to discover the truth for herself," Humbly offered in pointed tones.

It took a moment for Claredon to follow his subtle hint. When he did, his features twisted with distaste.

Of course it would be better if Victoria accepted for herself that her feelings for Stice were no more than those of caring woman for a weak man. But to actually encourage her to spend time with Stice made his teeth clench in fury. "Bloody hell," he muttered, exasperated beyond all endurance.

Humbly raised his brows. "Pardon me?"

"You are no doubt right, but I would far prefer the satisfaction of blackening the man's eye."

Humbly regarded him with a steady gaze. "Believe in your wife, my lord. You will not be disappointed."

He wished he could believe the kindly vicar. But until Victoria accepted him as her husband, his faith was in short supply. How could he trust her when she had no reason to feel the need to remain loyal to him? Oh, not in the physical sense, he acknowledged. He did not believe for a moment that her own honor would allow her to give her body to another man. But as he had said to the vicar, he could not dismiss the fear that she would allow the arrival of Mr. Stice to drive an even greater barrier between them.

"I hope you are right, Humbly," he said in low tones.

The vicar opened his mouth, no doubt to insist that Claredon agree that Victoria was above suspicion, but before he could speak, the door to the library was once again pushed open, this time to reveal the hesitant form of Claredon's wife.

Claredon ridiculously found himself closely inspecting her slender form, as if attempting to discover some sign of distress at having come face to face with the man she professed to love. He could discover nothing, however, beyond a certain pallor to her countenance and an uncertainty in her manner.

"Come in, my dear," he said in what he hoped were reassuring tones.

She stepped forward and glanced toward the silent vicar. "Good morning, Mr. Humbly."

"Good morning, Victoria. I was just on my way to breakfast. Shall I see you later?"

"Oh yes, of course," she readily agreed.

"Good." With a meaningful glance at Claredon the older gentleman politely slipped from the room, leaving him alone with his wife.

Claredon forced himself to take a deep breath before speaking. "Has Mr. Stice taken his leave so soon?"

Her hands clenched together as she determinedly lifted her gaze to meet his own. "No, he is still in the parlor."

"Is there a problem?"

"Actually . . ." Her words trailed away, and she visibly gathered her courage. "He has asked to remain for a few days."

Sharp disbelief raced through Claredon. "Here?"

"Yes."

Unable to accept that even Stice could possess the audacity to request to remain beneath the roof of his former fiancée and her new husband, Claredon abruptly turned to pace toward the window that overlooked the tidy gardens. "I see."

"I realize that you do not particularly care for Thomas," she said in carefully controlled tones, "but he truly does not have anywhere to go."

Claredon had several suggestions as to where the annoying twit could go, but the memory of the vicar's stern warnings held his tongue. "And you believe that I should allow the gentleman you claim to love remain beneath my roof?" he said in chilled tones.

There was a discomforting silence before Victoria cleared her throat. "I am well aware that Thomas can never be more than a friend."

He gave a humorless laugh. "Feelings are not so easily controlled as that."

She gave an impatient click of her tongue at his mocking tone. "You are determined to make this difficult, are you not?"

He was making this difficult? He turned to face her with an expression of annoyance. Damn and blast. How the devil would she feel if he requested that a former mistress become a houseguest?

Perhaps the vicar was right in that she should learn the truth of her emotions toward Stice on her own, but he was not above pointing out a few pertinent details she had seemed to overlook. He planted his hands upon his hips and stabbed her with a steely gaze. "Tell me, Victoria, has it occurred to you that it is rather odd that Mr. Stice has decided to make an unexpected appearance at this precise moment?"

She gave a bewildered shake of her head. "What do you mean?"

His lips twisted at her innocence. "First a scoundrel attempts to slip into our home. Then he threatens you and takes a shot at me. When it is obvious he has not been able to frighten us into giving him these mysterious jewels, Mr. Stice arrives upon our doorstep requesting to stay for a few days."

Not surprisingly, she stiffened at his blatant accusation of her beloved Thomas. "Are you implying that Thomas is involved with Mr. Smith?"

"Perhaps he *is* Mr. Smith," he retorted in silky tones. "The sketch you drew bears a resemblance to him."

Expecting anger, he was rather surprised when she instead appeared almost wary. "Absurd."

He stepped closer, resenting her ready defense of Stice more than he cared to acknowledge. "It makes perfect sense. He could not discover these jewels by force, so he has decided to slip in under the disguise of friendship."

"No." She gave a sharp shake of her head. "The man who accosted me in the carriage was not Thomas."

"How can you be so certain?" he persisted with a relentless expression. "You said yourself he was hidden by a scarf and cape."

Stubborn as ever, she refused to admit that Stice could be capable of such a nefarious plot. "I would have recognized him had it been Thomas."

Realizing he would be wasting his breath to insist that she had been too startled and frightened at the time to recognize her own mother, he gave a vague shrug. "Then perhaps he is using an accomplice."

"You are being ridiculous." Twisting her fingers together until he feared they might become irretrievably tangled, Victoria abruptly turned to pace away from his piercing gaze. "In the first place, there are no jewels to be found here, and in the second, Thomas would never be involved in anything remotely criminal."

Battling the urge to damn Thomas Stice to the netherworld, Claredon watched his wife with a growing suspicion. Her defense of Stice was almost too fierce. "Are you quite certain that he never gave you any jewels as an engagement gift?" he demanded.

"Yes."

"He never gave you any gifts?" he persisted.

She gave an impatient lift of one shoulder. "Only a trifling figurine."

Claredon frowned, refusing to accept that he was completely off the mark. Perhaps he did wish to think the worst of the annoying gentleman, but there was still the fact that he had arrived at the same moment that the trouble at Longmeade had begun. That could not be simply dismissed.

Or at least he did not desire to dismiss it.

"There must be something," he muttered. "This cannot be a mere coincidence."

"It cannot be Thomas. It cannot be. I will not believe it."

Suddenly certain that Victoria was hiding something from him, Claredon moved to lay his hands upon her shoulders and firmly turned her about. "Victoria, look at me," he commanded softly.

There was a moment's pause, as if she were debating ignoring his words. Then, with obvious reluctance, her long lashes fluttered upward to reveal troubled emerald eyes. "What?"

"There is something you are not telling me."

She wet her lips in a manner he was swiftly learning indicated she was nervous. "It is nothing."

"Victoria," he said in warning tones.

Her eyes darkened at his refusal to be dismissed. "It is only that Thomas mentioned something of his mother's jewels missing."

"Good God," he breathed in surprise.

Clearly anxious to ensure that he did not overreact to her confession, she reached up to grasp his hands with her own. Despite his smoldering anger, Claredon felt a rush of pleasure at the feel of her silky skin against his own.

"Claredon, it simply is not possible. Thomas is a weak man in many ways, but I have never known him to be dishonest. Indeed, he cannot tell the smallest lie without stammering and blushing a bright red."

"Perhaps you do not know him as well as you think you do," he retorted in harsh tones.

A wounded expression darkened her eyes, and Claredon swiftly regretted his urge to lash out at her perverse determination to protect her former fiancé. Dash it all! He had never concerned himself with whether a woman was singularly devoted to him before. In truth, the occasional mistress who had attempted to make him jealous had merely discovered herself dismissed in disgust at such a childish ploy. He had always presumed that he was above such a tedious emotion. After all, there were plenty of women awaiting his discovery.

Now he reluctantly realized that he could be just

as susceptible as the next man, a knowledge that did nothing to improve his temper.

Pulling away from him, Victoria wrapped her arms about her waist. "I think it more likely you are attempting to believe the worst because you do not like Thomas," she accused.

He heaved a weary sigh. "No, I do not like him. If you want the truth, I am jealous as hell of him."

She gave a choked sound at his blunt honesty, her expression bewildered. "Jealous?"

A rueful grimace twisted his lips. She seemed to find his confession as difficult to believe as he did.

"He managed to win your wary affection with inept ease, while I have struggled for months in vain." His hand rose of its own violation to allow his fingers to gently touch the soft temptation of her full lips. "He appears to know the way to your heart."

He felt her tremble beneath his gentle caress, but she did not pull away.

"You certainly have not attempted to win my affection," she denied in uneven tones. "You are forever provoking me."

"Would you have been swayed by soft words?" he challenged with a lift of his brows. "You have been determined to hate me since we were wed."

Astonishingly, her eyes widened as if she were shocked by his accusation. Or perhaps she simply had not allowed herself to put words to her determined dislike. "That is not true," she breathed softly. "I do not hate you."

"No?"

"Of course not."

Claredon experienced a ridiculous warmth flare through his heart at her adamant denial. Perhaps there was hope for them yet. "Then what do you feel, Victoria?" he asked softly.

"I . . ." She swallowed heavily, her gaze abruptly dropping as if seeking to hide her inner confusion. "This is hardly the time for such a discussion."

He smiled wryly at her ready retreat. Gads, she was as elusive as the fog, near enough to see and feel, but never able to be grasped. Unable to help himself, he stepped forward and wrapped his arms about her waist, jerking her satisfyingly close to the aching hardness of his body. "And when will be the proper time for such a discussion?" he rasped.

Her head jerked upward as her hands raised to press against the coiled muscles of his chest. "Claredon."

"You have not answered my question."

A bewitching bewilderment fluttered over her countenance, making Claredon's arms tighten. She felt so very right pressed against him, soft and so enchantingly vulnerable. He would not lose her to the lure of a gentleman who could never be more than a selfish burden, he swore to himself silently. She deserved better than that.

Besides, a possessive voice whispered in the back of his mind, she belonged to him, and he intended to do whatever necessary to keep her.

"We were discussing Thomas," she breathed in uneven tones.

"I prefer to discuss us," he said with a soft persistence, his fingers lightly tracing the delicious curve of her spine. "Last night I had begun to hope that you were beginning to care for me. You appeared so upset that I had been injured."

She arched beneath the soft caress of his hand,

pressing her body even more firmly against his own. Claredon swallowed an instinctive growl of pleasure.

"Of course I was upset," she forced herself to say as she battled the shimmering heat that flared between them.

"Because you care?" he demanded, all too conscious of the sofa only a few feet away. With one movement he could have her swept off her feet and lying back on the soft cushions. It was small, but he was growing desperate enough to overcome any obstacle. Of course, there was much to be said for the nearby desk, he fuzzily acknowledged. He could place her upon the edge and . . .

"Because you're my husband." She broke into his lurid thoughts.

He gave a slow shake of his head, refusing to believe her desperate anger of the night before was mere duty. "And you care," he insisted in velvet rough tones.

Her eyes briefly fluttered closed as his seeking hands cupped her hips and cradled her firmly to his lower body. "I suppose."

He felt a stab of frustration at her grudging tone. She proclaimed her love for Stice with glorious ease. Why could she not admit even the smallest hint of affection for him without behaving as if she was having a tooth drawn? "Is that so terribly difficult to say, Victoria?" he demanded in sharp tones. "Am I such a horrid person that it grieves you to feel a glimmer of kindness for me?"

She abruptly lifted her gaze to reveal haunted eyes. "I did not wish to feel anything for you."

He flinched as if she had slapped him. Although he had always known she was determined to keep barriers between them, he had not actually heard the words fall from her lips.

Now he wanted to howl out in frustration.

They had both been forced to give up their hopes and plans for their future. He had lost as much as she. Surely she could see that it was only sensible that they discover new plans that included one another. They could do better than this constant fighting and bickering.

His thoughts strayed back to the nearby desk. Much, much better than this.

"Victoria . . ." The unwelcome voice abruptly shattered the silence of the library, causing Victoria to leap out of Claredon's arms at the same moment Mr. Stice enter the room. Claredon bristled with instant antagonism, not bothering to hide his displeasure as the intruder stumbled to a halt at the sight of his grim countenance. "Oh . . . my lord."

Claredon flexed his fingers, wanting nothing so much as to wrap them about the man's scrawny neck. "Stice," he muttered between clenched teeth.

At least the dimwit had the intelligence to shift uneasily beneath his feral stare. "I merely wished to thank Victoria again for allowing me to remain at Longmeade," he stammered.

Claredon opened his mouth to inform the fool that not only was he not welcome at Longmeade, but that he would be well served to flee before he found himself drowned in the nearby cove. But the sudden sensation of Victoria's pleading gaze locked onto him halted the impetuous warning.

Bloody hell.

If he tossed Stice from the estate, he would no doubt be branded an unfeeling monster, even if he were the one in the right. Not only would Victoria accuse him of not trusting her, but she would stubbornly use her grievance as yet another reason to keep them apart. He was well and truly damned if he did and damned if he didn't, he angrily acknowledged. "I trust that you have been made comfortable?" he managed to choke out with a semblance of manners.

The younger man bobbed his head up and down. "Oh yes, quite comfortable."

"Good."

Stice coughed, wisely backing toward the still open door. "Ah . . . well . . . I must change before luncheon. If you will excuse me?"

Not bothering to wait for a response, the coward turned to bolt back through the door. Claredon could not deny a faint flare of satisfaction at his swift flight. Perhaps the idiot did possess a bit of sense.

"You will allow him to remain?" Victoria demanded in obvious surprise.

Turning to regard his baffled wife, Claredon smoothed his features into an unreadable expression. He was not about to admit to Victoria that he feared her reaction if he did not give in to her demands. Such power was far too dangerous to hand over easily. "Oh yes, he will remain," he said in smooth tones. "I intend to keep a very close guard on Mr. Stice."

Her nose flared with irritation at his explanation. "Really, Claredon, you are impossible."

"No, I am determined." He reached out to grasp her chin in a firm grip. "I never play to lose, my dear. You might want to remember that."

Ten

The week had been intolerable.

Victoria heaved a sigh as she absently crumbled a slice of toast onto her plate. She had not expected Claredon to be pleased by her insistence that Thomas be allowed to remain. In fact, she had been quite conscious that he would be angry at the thought of her former fiancé staying beneath his roof. But she had not expected the icily aloof manner that seemed to fill the household with an uncomfortable chill.

He was no longer the teasing flirt that he had been after Humbly's arrival, nor even the provoking adversary she had come to expect. Instead, he was remote and utterly unreachable.

Much to her dismay, Victoria discovered herself ruing the loss of his determined pursuit. Ridiculous, considering she had been terrified by the thought of succumbing to his practiced seduction. She should be celebrating his cold distance. But in truth, she felt a heavy sense of loss in her heart when he passed her in the hall with no more than a mere nod or sat at the dining table without ever seeming to note her presence.

Even worse, Thomas had proven to be a most demanding guest. It seemed she could not take a step without him at her side. From the moment she wakened until she at last retired to her chambers, he was incessantly seeking her company, filling the air with his meaningless chatter, and constantly fretting over his ill treatment at the hands of his mother.

More than once, Victoria had been forced to bite her tongue when his self-pity rasped against her nerves. How had she never noted how utterly self-consumed this man was, she silently wondered. Or how demanding he could be?

The truth of the matter was that Claredon had been right. She had not known Thomas as well as she should have, certainly not well enough to elope with him. And she was reluctantly beginning to acknowledge that it had been more pity than love that had urged her to reach out to the hapless gentleman.

Feeling utterly miserable, she reluctantly glanced across the table to where Thomas was busily consuming a large plate of food. Both Claredon and Mr. Humbly had wisely learned to avoid the breakfast room whenever Thomas entered. Treacherously, she realized that she wished she were in the position to do the same.

"I must tell you, Victoria, that I was quite insistent that I did not care for the buttons upon this waistcoat," he was saying with blithe indifference to her lack of attention. "But the tailor simply would not hear of changing them no matter how I pleaded."

Knowing she was wasting her breath, Victoria could not help but point out the obvious. "It is your waistcoat, Thomas. If you do not like the buttons, you should have them changed."

He appeared predictably scandalized by her simple solution. "Oh no, the man claimed that it would ruin the entire effect. I would not wish to have an awkward waistcoat."

Victoria heaved a sigh. "No, I suppose not."

Suddenly frowning, Thomas leaned forward. "What do you think?"

"I beg your pardon?"

"Of the buttons," he prompted. "Do you think I should have had them changed?"

"Oh." She gave an indifferent glance over the garish buttons, wondering why the devil she had gotten herself into this bumblebroth. Her husband was furious with her, poor Mr. Humbly had all but disappeared, and this gentleman was swiftly driving her to Bedlam. "They are fine buttons."

"They are not too large?"

"No, not at all."

Thomas abruptly heaved a sigh, as if his buttons were of paramount importance. "You put my mind greatly at ease, Victoria. It is so worrisome to make such decisions on my own. I far preferred when you would come with me and deal with such tedious details."

Victoria shivered, abruptly realizing how close she had come to being at this gentleman's constant behest. Good heavens, she never would have had a moment's peace nor a hope of pursuing her own interests. How could she, when she would have been forced to make every decision for Thomas? The unnerving realization twisted her stomach in knots.

Deciding that it was time she take matters in her own hands, Victoria determinedly squared her shoulders. Although she still did not believe that Thomas could possibly be involved with the dangerous Mr. Smith, she could not utterly deny that it was odd that his mother's jewels had gone missing at the same moment this man had appeared in Kent. Perhaps there was some connection that they could not yet determine.

Besides, she was ready at this point to discuss anything but buttons. "Thomas."

"Take these boots for example . . ." he continued without hearing her interruption. "I believe that I was quite shabbily taken by Hoby. If only you had been along, I am certain he . . ."

"Thomas," she repeated, loud enough he could not fail to note her determination.

Giving a mild blink, he regarded her with a questioning gaze. "Yes, my dear?"

"You told me that you had argued with your mother concerning her missing jewels."

A rather peevish expression settled on the youthful features at her sudden shift in conversation. "I would prefer not to recall that horrid argument."

"Of course," she forced herself to say in soothing tones. "But I have been thinking upon your troubles, and I wondered if it is possible that her jewels truly are missing?"

"It is all nonsense. Mother has merely misplaced them."

Victoria briefly thought of the loud, overbearing woman who ruled everyone and everything about her with an iron fist. "Forgive me, Thomas, but your mother does not seem the type to mislay a fortune in jewels."

He frowned. "She must have."

"You are quite convinced they were not stolen?"

Without warning Thomas tossed his napkin onto the table and pushed his plate away with a sulky motion. "Good God, Victoria, surely you would not believe I would steal my own mother's jewels."

"No, of course not," she assured him.

"I should hope not," he offered her a chastising glance. "Really, I have endured quite enough from Mother. To think you would also accuse me of something so heinous is really more than I can bear."

Victoria forced herself to count to ten. She had endured almost all she could bear, as well. "Have you considered the notion that someone else might have been responsible for the theft?"

Thomas settled back with a startled expression. "Who?"

"I do not know. When did your mother miss her jewels?"

He gave a restless shrug, as if disturbed by even discussing the unpleasant subject. "She claims that she noted their disappearance shortly after our . . . elopement. She presumed that I had taken them to pay for our journey to Scotland and she had hoped once I returned to London I would eventually return them."

His overt lack of concern for his mother's missing property stunned Victoria. "And you did not believe you should make an attempt to discover what happened to the jewels?"

A hint of embarrassment touched his face at her unconsciously chiding tone. "What could I do?"

"Well, at least you could have searched a few of the places she might have left them or questioned the servants."

"For goodness sakes, I was too furious to concern myself with discovering the jewels," he whined at her reasonable words. "Besides, I cannot be expected to be bothered with such things. My nerves are very delicate, you know, and easily overset."

She slowly gave a shake of her head. "But surely . . ."

"What?" he prompted as her words broke off.

"Never mind," she muttered, realizing that Thomas truly believed his nerves were too weak to allow him to do anything remotely unpleasant. A fine trick, if one could get by with it. "What shall we do today?"

Perfectly willing to set aside all discussion of the missing jewels, Thomas heaved a deep sigh. "I suppose I should write to Mother and tell her where I am."

"Of course."

"No matter how angry I might be, it would not do to worry her."

"No."

"Not that I have forgiven her, mind," he hastily added, as if worried that Victoria might consider him too tightly tied to the apron strings. "I shall demand an apology."

Victoria was past caring. "Of course."

"And I shall insist that she halt having me followed about like a child," he added as an afterthought.

"Most wise."

"I will be treated as an adult."

"Yes."

There was a long pause before Thomas regarded her with a pleading gaze. "Will you help me write the letter, Victoria? I am no good as such things."

"Oh, Thomas . . ." Her words broke off as a movement outside the window suddenly captured her attention. With a hasty motion she was on her feet and crossing to peer down at the gardens.

"What is it, Victoria?" Thomas demanded.

"My husband," she muttered, readily thrusting aside her thoughts of her annoying guest as she watched Claredon determinedly moving toward the distant stables. How dare he, she seethed. He had distinctly promised her that he would not leave the property without someone at his side. Well, he would not escape so easily.

Without a second thought she whirled on her heel and headed toward the door.

She halted briefly as Thomas rose to his feet with a frown. "Victoria, are you leaving me?"

"I must speak with Claredon."

"But what of my letter?" he complained in shrill tones.

The urge to tell him precisely what she thought of his absurd letter was hastily swallowed before she could tempt fate. Instead she forced a stiff smile to her lips. "I think it would be best if you wrote to your mother on your own."

"Oh no, I could not possibly . . ."

Victoria's patience could endure no more. She had truly attempted to be kind to Thomas, not only because of their past friendship, but, more importantly, to hide from Claredon the realization that he had been so horribly right.

She would have been miserable tied to the childish man. More than that, she would have been a virtual prisoner to his endless demands. Her pride, however, had demanded that she hide her disillusionment from the one gentleman who seemed to know her better than she knew herself.

Now she had more important thoughts upon her mind than pacifying Thomas or even hiding her changing feelings from Claredon.

Moving at a near run, she flew down the stairs and out the door the butler barely managed to pull open in time. From there she angled directly toward the stables to step into Claredon's path as he left the gardens. "Claredon."

He came to a startled halt at her sudden appearance, his expression swiftly smoothing to unreadable lines. "Good morning, Victoria."

"Where are you going?" she demanded in sharp tones.

Not surprisingly, his lips twisted at her peremptory manner, a faintly mocking glint entering his eyes.

"Good morning, Claredon," he said in sardonic tones. "How did you sleep? Well, I hope. How handsome you appear on this fine day."

Only days ago his provoking words would have sent her into a fury. Today, however, she found a ridiculous glow of happiness enter her heart at his taunting. Anything, anything was preferable to that cold aloofness.

"Forgive me," she said with a faint smile. "How did you sleep?"

His eyes swiftly darkened as he glanced down at her simple muslin gown, which was molded to her curves by the summer breeze. "Very poorly."

She frowned in concern, unaware that the sunlight filtering through the thin fabric offered a tantalizing outline of her slender body. "Is your shoulder troubling you?"

He drew in a deep breath. "You know quite well what is troubling me, my love."

Victoria could not halt the sudden rush of color that filled her cheeks, nor her instinctive desire to shift the conversation to less dangerous topics. "You have not told me where you are going."

He smiled wryly at her swift retreat, but thankfully followed her lead. "Lord Vernon has a field that marches with our land that he is considering selling. I wished to familiarize myself with it before making an offer."

She planted her hands on her hips and regarded him in a stern fashion.

"Alone?"

He shrugged. "It is not far."

"You made me a promise," she reminded him.

With deliberate movements, he crossed his arms over the width of his chest and regarded her with a brooding gaze. "I did, indeed, but I must admit that I did not presume you would thank me for dragging you away from your precious Mr. Stice."

"He is not my precious Mr. Stice," she informed him tartly. "He is simply a friend in need of my help."

"What he is in need of is a backbone," he muttered in disgust.

Not at all anxious to discuss Thomas or his disruptive presence in their household, Victoria tilted her chin to a determined angle. "If you will give me a few moments, I will change into my habit."

His brows arched in disbelief. "You intend to join me?"

"I do not wish you to be on your own."

"What of Mr. Stice?"

She heaved an impatient sigh. "Will you wait?"

His gaze openly roamed over her upturned countenance before a worrisome smile curved his lips. "Forever, if need be, Victoria."

Her breath seemed to be sucked from her body at his low words. Just for a moment she wondered if she was being completely wise in deliberately seeking time alone with her husband. Did she not already know how vulnerable she was becoming to his persuasive seduction? Had she not already accepted that she cared far more than she had ever intended? Was she not increasingly aware that her supposed love for

Thomas was no more than a fraud that could no longer protect her heart?

The thoughts swiftly passed through her mind, only to be easily dismissed.

Although they had seen nor heard anything of Mr. Smith in the past week, it did not mean the danger had disappeared. She would not allow Claredon to risk himself again. "I will be only a few moments."

With a resigned shake of his head, Claredon continued his path to the stables to have their mounts saddled. Dash it all, he had been determined to remain stoically composed when in the presence of his wife. It was bad enough to have Stice connected to her side like a leech, without him storming about like a jealous fool.

She would never suspect that he had every servant in the household keeping a careful watch on their movements, he had told himself. Or that he spent his nights pacing the floor, consumed with the dark need to gather her from her room and place her in his bed, where she belonged.

He would simply pretend to above such childish emotions.

Eventually he would catch the gentleman in the act of something devious, or more likely the fool would simply crawl back to his mother. In either case, he would be gone from Longmeade and Victoria would have to accept that her life was here with him.

At least he could hope for such an outcome if he did not ruin it all by infuriating Victoria beyond forgiveness.

Shaking his head, Claredon led the horses to the courtyard. Perhaps it was beyond hope to remain aloof from his wife. The moment she was in his presence, he was assaulted by a myriad of emotions—impatience, lust, and the oddest sense of tenderness. He was torn between wanting to toss her upon the nearest bed and holding her in his arms to protect her from the world.

Such confusion was bound to make him crazed, he assured himself wryly. For the moment all he could do was hold onto the knowledge that she at least worried over him. It was a beginning.

He discovered Victoria awaiting him in the courtyard attired in a lovely cinnamon habit, and after helping her into her saddle, he mounted his own horse. "Are you ready?" he demanded.

"Yes."

"Then let us be off." Urging his horse down the path that would lead across the parkland, he covertly studied the woman who had haunted his thoughts for far too long. She rode well, moving with a lithe grace that was incredibly enticing. Too enticing, he acknowledged as he wrenched his gaze toward the distant tree line. "I trust Mr. Humbly will keep Mr. Stice suitably entertained?"

"Mr. Humbly is visiting our local rector, while Thomas is writing a letter to his mother."

"Ah, the dutiful son," he mocked before he could halt the words.

He was swiftly punished for his impulse as she sent him a flashing gaze. "Do you intend to be provoking for the entire morning?" she demanded in exasperation.

"Absolutely not." He slowed his horse, gazing deep into her wary eyes. "It is far too rare for me to have you all to myself. I intend to be on my best behavior."

Thankfully, her lips gave a reluctant twitch at his

solemn promise. "Why do I find that difficult to believe?"

"I haven't the least notion."

She shook her head before attempting about distract his unwavering gaze. "Have you discovered any further information about Mr. Smith?"

His lips briefly tightened at the unwelcome reminder that he had not yet found a trace of the scoundrel. Even calling in the magistrate had not turned up any clues. "Nothing beyond the fact that he has not returned to the inn since the night he attempted to do away with me."

"Perhaps he was frightened when he discovered he had wounded you. He might very well have fled Kent," she suggested.

Claredon was not nearly so certain. It was just as likely the culprit had decided to send Stice to the house to search for the jewels while he laid low.

This time, however, he possessed the wisdom to hold his tongue. "Perhaps," he murmured. "I still wish you to take care until we have gotten to the bottom of this trouble."

"If you will recall, you were the one attempting to sneak away on your own," she retorted in pointed tones.

"As I said, I did not believe you would desire to be interrupted." Claredon paused, cautiously considering his words. He ached to know precisely what Victoria felt of Stice's arrival at Longmeade at the same moment he feared her response. A fine dilemma for a gentleman who had always preferred casual, temporary affairs to the complications of relationships. "Have you enjoyed Mr. Stice's visit?"

Her hands abruptly clenched upon her reins until her mount tossed his head in protest. With an obvious effort, she loosened her grip and even managed a thin smile. "It is always nice to see an old friend," she said in determinedly bland tones.

Instantly intrigued, Claredon shifted closer, watching her features for any sign of her inner thoughts. "He was more than a mere friend."

She deliberately studied the well-scythed parkland, almost as if determined to avoid his gaze. "I thought you promised not to try and provoke me," she accused.

"I am not attempting to be provoking for once," he assured her. "I do not believe that anything improper has occurred since his arrival. I am merely interested in how you are bearing to be with the man you once loved now that he is beyond your reach."

There was a taut silence before she gave a restless shrug. "It has been . . . difficult."

Claredon felt as if he had been punched in the gut. "Your feelings toward Stice have not altered?"

"I would really prefer not to discuss the subject, Claredon."

His features tightened as that horrid wave of jealously rushed through him. Gads, he was surely being repaid for a lifetime of frivolous affairs. "I do not mean to distress you, Victoria, but I would think as your husband I have a right to know if you are still attached to one another."

Her tongue peeked out to wet her lips before she at last responded to his low command. "I suppose my feelings have somewhat altered."

"In what way?"

"I . . ." She heaved an exasperated sigh. "I have begun to wonder if I had not been mistaken in Thomas."

As swiftly as the jealousy had attacked, it was abruptly pierced by a shaft of hope. "Mistaken?"

She still refused to meet his searching gaze, but Claredon did not miss the tension etched upon her features. Clearly something was troubling her. "When we were together in London, it was for only very brief visits, and those were usually marred by his overbearing mother. She was so determined to see him wed to an heiress that she did everything possible to keep us apart."

Claredon smiled wryly. "Thereby ensuring that your meetings were secretive and spiced with the pleasure of outwitting her?"

She sent him a startled glance. "Yes."

He gave a shake of his head. "It never fails to amaze me that those determined to keep lovers apart persistently do the things that are bound to bring them together. Few of us can resist the forbidden. And, of course, by keeping a couple separated, it allows them to weave the most ridiculous fantasies, rather than seeing each other as they truly are."

Victoria drew in a deep breath. "I had little opportunity to fully understand Thomas's nature, or to question his reasons for wishing to be with me."

"And now?" he prompted softly, unconsciously holding his breath as she reluctantly met his gaze.

"Now I realize that I never loved him."

Eleven

Victoria averted her gaze and stared grimly ahead as the taut silence stretched to an almost unbearable length.

It had not been a simple matter to confess the truth to Claredon. Not only did she appear a fool for so grievously mistaking her tepid sympathy for love, but she had lowered one of the stiff barriers that kept her husband at bay. Now that she could no longer hide behind her loyal feelings for Thomas, it left her vulnerable and decidedly ill at ease.

Still, she discovered herself unable to lie any longer. Claredon had proven to be far more loyal and dependable than she had ever allowed herself to hope. He had risked his life to ensure her safety, something Thomas never would have considered. He deserved to have the truth, if nothing else.

For what seemed to be an eternity there was only the rustle of leaves and the distant sound of dogs barking as they entered the thick woods ringing the property.

Then, bringing his mount even closer to her own, he studied her features with an oddly intense gaze. "I see," he at long last murmured.

"I care for him as a friend, of course," she hastily

said, unable to halt the faint flare of panic that raced through her.

"Of course."

She wetted her dry lips, almost able to feel his probing gaze as it watched her betraying movement. "And I do wish to help him stand up to his mother. No gentleman should be so easily browbeaten."

There was another faint pause. "Victoria?"

"Yes?"

"Will you look at me?" he demanded softly.

She slowly drew in a deep breath before forcing herself to turn and meet his searching gaze. For a breathless moment, she felt lost in the impossible blue of his eyes. They seemed so compellingly tender and filled with gentle understanding that her heart nearly melted.

"How can you be so certain of your feelings?" he asked, his voice oddly uneven. "You believed you loved him for a very long time, and it has been only a week since he arrived."

"I . . . I think I was more in love with the notion of being in love," she reluctantly answered, barely paying heed to the narrow path they were following. "You were right when you said that I was very lonely after Anne wed. She had been so much a part of my life I suppose I did not precisely know what to do with myself when she no longer needed me."

Thankfully, he showed no arrogance at her grudging admittance that he had been right all along. Instead, a gentle smile curved his lips. "So you found a new cause to sponsor?"

Victoria thought back to her determined support of Thomas and her rather shameful delight in besting his mother. In retrospect, it appeared more a challenge of her skills at helping another than a true courtship. "Yes." She gave a lift of her shoulder. "Thomas was so helpless and incapable of defending himself I naturally attempted to assist him."

"Perfectly understandable, Victoria," he said in low tones. "You have a very caring heart. It is what I admire most about you."

Victoria could not help the pleased blush that rose to her cheeks. Despite the knowledge that any successful rogue must have a smooth tongue, she felt as susceptible as any other maiden to his flattery. "I feel like a naive fool," she said, in an effort to distract him.

"Do not."

She raised her brows in surprise at his suddenly sharp words. "What?"

His gaze narrowed. "Never apologize for your giving nature. If we all possessed such kindness, it would be a far better world."

Victoria caught her breath. A smooth tongue, indeed. "That is easy for you to say." She attempted to ease the suddenly thick atmosphere. "I doubt you ever mistook sympathy for love."

Without warning, his lips twisted in a self-derisive fashion. "Perhaps not, but I do know what it is like to be disillusioned when I discovered a person I cared for could not live up to the image I had created."

It took her a long moment to realize what he meant by the cryptic words. Then a twinge of sympathy plucked at her heart. "Your father?"

"Yes." The old but lingering disappointment could be detected deep in his eyes. "When I was young, I put him on a pedestal. He was handsome, charming, and such a wonderful father I thought no gentleman could possibly equal him."

Victoria offered him an understanding smile. She was very aware that it was not easy for him to confess his long held sense of betrayal, and she found herself deeply touched that he possessed enough faith in her to speak of his distress. "When did you discover the truth?"

He abruptly turned his head to study the path ahead of them. No doubt he was as reluctant as she to reveal his vulnerability.

"I suppose I always knew that he enjoyed the company of other women," he slowly admitted. "He rarely made a secret of his visits to the village, where he sought to seduce whatever pretty maiden captured his attention. But not until I awakened early one morning and watched my father slip into the house did I witness my mother standing in the door to her bedchamber with tears running down her face. I realized then just how deeply my mother felt my father's betrayal."

Victoria experienced a flare of fury at Claredon's father. How could he possibly treat his wife with such disrespect? And, more importantly, how could he disappoint his adoring son? She could easily sense that Claredon had been devastated at the realization his father was not the paragon he had thought. And perhaps even torn between loyalty to the man he loved and the mother who was being hurt. It was a horrid position to put a child in.

"Did you ever confront your father?" she asked in cautious tones, not wanting to push his confidences, but eager to know more of this man she called husband.

His features hardened in an alarming manner. "Once, when I was seventeen. My mother had just been approached by a local barmaid, who demanded money for the child she was carrying that belonged to my father. I overheard the confrontation and was furious that my mother had been put into such an embarrassing situation."

"What did your father do?"

"He laughed." A barely perceptible tremor raced through Claredon's elegant form. "In his opinion, the local women were there for his amusement, and my mother was being overly sensitive to be hurt by his infidelities. He said that he loved his wife, but no gentleman could be expected to remain faithful."

Victoria was shocked in spite of herself. Her own father had adored her mother. There had never been the slightest hint he would ever desire another. And, in truth, her mother was precisely the sort of woman who would have greeted her errant husband at the door with a heavy vase upside his head, rather than tears.

"But you did not believe him," she said, with more than a hint of satisfaction.

He smiled wryly at her less than subtle disgust toward Lord Moreland. "No. I called him an unfeeling lout and promptly bloodied his nose."

"Good heavens."

"It took a while to mend our estrangement. In fact, it was only the realization that my anger toward Father was deeply distressing my mother that forced me to put aside our differences."

Victoria gave a shake of her head, not at all certain she could have been so gracious in a similar situation. No doubt it was best for the family not to have Claredon and his father at odds, but it would not be easy to turn a blind eye to such betrayal. "Your mother sounds like a very wonderful and brave woman," she said softly.

He abruptly turned to face her, his features softening with undeniable love for his mother. "She is, indeed. Although she had eight children to raise, she always managed to make each of us feel special."

"And shamelessly spoiled you," she teased.

He gave a sudden laugh. "But of course. Tell me of your parents."

Caught off guard by his sudden request, Victoria gave a shake of her head. "There is little to tell. We lived quietly at our estate. My father was a farmer at heart, and my mother possessed little interest in Society. I do remember that they always seemed to be a great deal in love. Every morning my father would awaken my mother with a newly bloomed rose."

"Ah, a romantic," he retorted.

A reminiscent smile curved her lips at the memory of her father's gentle nature and love of books. "Yes, I believe he was."

His gaze swept over her countenance, lingering for a disturbing moment upon her lips. "And you hoped someday to marry a gentleman as devoted as your father?"

Although it had never been a conscious thought, she realized now that she had indeed harbored a deep hope she would one day be as loved as her mother had been. How would it feel to have a gentleman gaze at her with wonder? To treat her as if she were a rare gift he could never quite believe he had won?

The knowledge she would never know made a faint ache open in her heart. "I suppose," she said slowly.

As if sensing her sudden cloud of regret, Claredon reached over to slowly stroke her cheek. "I am sorry, Victoria."

She glanced at him in surprise. "Why?"

He heaved a sigh. "You are a woman who deserves a gentleman you can truly love. A marriage of convenience will never satisfy you."

She gave a restless shrug, not wishing to dwell upon the future. It made her long for things she could never possess.

"As Vicar Humbly says, we are not always given the paths we would chose," she said in attempt at forbearance. Her fate had been decided, and all she could do was make the best of it.

Claredon gave a rueful grimace. "Ah, yes. I received a similar sermon."

Victoria determinedly put on a brave face. "And I cannot wholly deny that our unfortunate incident did rescue me from marriage to Thomas."

"There is that," he murmured. Then, without warning, he pulled his horse to a sudden halt and glanced about him.

Instantly on alert, Victoria regarded him with alarm. "What is it?"

"I had almost forgotten," he retorted with a mysterious smile. "I have something I wish you to see."

"Here?"

Slipping off his horse, Claredon tossed the reins over a nearby branch. Then, approaching her, he held up his arms to offer her assistance. "Come along, Victoria. You can trust me."

For a moment Victoria gazed down at his waiting arms.

You can trust me . . .

Claredon was uncertain why he had uttered the words, but now he discovered himself holding his breath as she wavered between retreating behind her fierce walls of protection and allowing herself to accept what he wished to offer.

Suddenly he realized this moment was about more

than simply helping her dismount. It was a turning point in their relationship. She could either push him away or dare to allow him closer.

Thick silence seemed to surround them as Victoria briefly glanced about the trees that isolated them from the rest of the world. Then, just when he feared she was about to demand they continue on to inspect the land, she gave a hesitant nod. "Very well."

Feeling a rush of jubilation, Claredon wrapped his hands about her tiny waist and swung her to the ground.

The tantalizing scent of lilacs briefly teased at his nose as he reluctantly loosened his hold and turned about to lead her off the path. The feel of her beneath his fingers had suddenly wakened the ever ready desire that he had stoically buried during the past week. He could not help but wonder if he wasn't making a mistake. Having her alone was perhaps not the wisest choice, if the merest touch could make his stomach clench with fierce, burning need.

With an effort, Claredon shook his head and continued toward the large tree that lay straight ahead. He had waited a week to spend just a few moments with his wife. He wasn't about to ruin their precious time together because he was consumed by lust.

He was not his father.

Halting beneath the wide, spreading branches of the tree, he reached up to grasp one of the lower limbs and, with the ease of years of practice, swung himself upward.

Below him, he heard Victoria give a startled gasp. "Claredon, what are you doing?"

"Just wait a moment," he urged, swiftly using the branches to climb ever upward.

"Good heavens, you are going to break your neck!"

He chuckled as he reached the large wooden planks that surrounded a perfect cottage hidden in the thick foliage.

"I am not yet so old I cannot climb a tree or two," he complained, walking over the wooden floor to collect the ladder lying beside the door to the cottage. Moving toward the edge, he began to lower it downward. "Stand back. I am going to give you some help." Feeling the ladder hit the ground below, he carefully held onto the top rung. "Can you climb up?"

"I am not yet so old that I cannot climb a ladder." She threw his words back at him in tart tones.

Knowing it would help that she had on her habit, Claredon still peered anxiously downward as he spotted her pale champagne bonnet peeking through the leaves. "Be careful."

"Really, Claredon . . ." She began to protest, only to have her words stolen as she climbed past the boards and spotted the pretty house set in the bower of limbs. "Oh, what is this?"

Pulling her onto the boards, Claredon regarded her with a teasing smile. "Until my grandfather's death, we lived at this estate. The house was not all that large, and with seven older sisters my father realized I needed a place to escape from their constant mothering. He had this secretly built so that I could hide when it became unbearable."

Her brows lifted. "Your own private cottage?"

"Believe me, with seven sisters it was more a necessity than an extravagance," he assured her, turning to run his hand over the top of one windowsill. "Now, where did I . . . ah, here it is."

Taking the key he had just located, Claredon swiftly unlocked the door and opened it so that he could usher Victoria inside. With a faint grimace at the smell of neglected dust and disuse that filled the shadowed air, he glanced about the single room that had been such a wonderful part of his childhood.

In one corner were the wide sofa and chair that had been taken from the attics of Longmeade, along with a writing desk where he had spent endless hours writing wretchedly horrid poetry. Closer to the window was a telescope he had used to survey the land below when he was pretending to be a pirate protecting his stash of treasure. It was all fairly rustic when seen through the eyes of an adult, but when he was younger it was a haven beyond measure.

"This is your hideaway?" Victoria demanded as she gazed about the cramped room.

"I fear it has been sadly neglected," he apologized as he noted the cobwebs that glittered in the streaming sunlight.

She flashed him a wry smile as she moved toward the center of the barren floor. "I would say that it was in better condition than most cottages in England."

Hearing a faint creak, Claredon frowned as he hurried forward. "Do not move until I have ensured that the boards are still steady," he commanded, gingerly pacing back and forth across the room until he was certain none of the boards had rotted during his long absence. "They seem secure enough," he at last conceded.

Obviously curious to discover more of his nefarious childhood, Victoria strolled aimlessly toward the writing desk. "Your sisters never discovered your secret?"

"Never," he said, recalling the elaborate means he would use to throw off anyone who might be following him before ever approaching his secret cottage. "Not even my mother knew of it."

"What would you do here?"

Claredon felt a faint hint of embarrassment at discussing his youthful fantasies. "When I was younger, I would pretend I was a pirate and this was my ship, or that I was knight in his castle."

Thankfully, her smile held nothing but a sweet teasing at his confession. "How very dashing."

He waggled his brows in a wicked manner. "Oh, I assure you I was quite dashing."

"And when you were older?"

He gave a faint grimace as he moved to join her at the writing table. Once again, he was dangerously aware of the heat and tempting scent of her skin. The urge to reach out and touch her was nearly unbearable. "I am not certain I wish to confess," he murmured, barely paying heed to his offhand words until she abruptly stiffened.

"I suppose you used it to seduce all the local maids," she said in unnaturally brittle tones.

He abruptly frowned, oddly hurt by her swift assumption he devoted all his time to seducing women. Ridiculous, of course. Why wouldn't she suspect the worst? He had spent far too much time in the pursuit of pleasure.

But he discovered he did not want his wife thinking of him as a lecherous rogue. He wanted her trust. Her belief that he would never harm her. "You could not be more wrong, Victoria," he said in tones more sharp than he intended. "I assure you that I have never seduced any woman here."

She abruptly flushed with embarrassment. "Oh."

Ruing the sudden discord between them, Claredon reached down to pull the top of the writing desk upward, and collected the large sheaf of papers that had been hidden inside. Not giving himself time for second thoughts, he abruptly shoved them into Victoria's hands. "Here."

Startled by his sudden movements, she regarded him with wide eyes. "What are these?"

His lips twisted with wry humor. "The shockingly odious poetry I use to write when I was a young man."

She regarded him for a long moment before at last lowering her head to read through the scribbled lines upon the pages.

Claredon found himself barely resisting the urge to turn away as she read through the very private outpouring of emotions that he had placed on the paper.

Being young and foolish, he had not attempted to hide his deep yearning for true love, nor his innocent belief in a maiden who would fill his life with joy.

It seemed an eternity before she slowly lifted her head to regard him with glowing eyes. His heart tripped as she reached out to lightly touch his arm. "Claredon . . . these are beautiful."

A ridiculous sense of pleasure washed through him even as he gave an embarrassed shake of his head. "Good lord, they are ghastly."

Her hand tightened upon his arm as she moved close enough for his body to tingle with sudden anticipation. Dear heavens, he had made love to her a hundred times in his dreams and now she was so near, and they were so alone . . . .

He shuddered as he battled his inner demons.

"I like them very much, Claredon," she was saying softly. "Why did you stop writing?"

He forced himself to shrug. "I had no desire to become a rather poor imitation of Byron. One melancholy poet in Society is quite enough."

She refused to be put off by his dismissive tone,

that familiar stubborn expression descending upon her lovely features. "You should have them published."

"No. Absolutely not," he retorted, firmly taking the papers from her hands and tossing them back in the writing desk. "To be honest, I never expected to share them with anyone."

"Why?" she persisted.

He heaved a rueful sigh. "I suppose it is rather like baring one's soul. It is an uncomfortable feeling."

Her expression slowly softened at his words, a rather wistful smile touching her lips. "I am glad that you shared them with me."

Unable to resist temptation any longer, Claredon carefully reached up to cup her cheek. "You are my wife. There should be nothing we cannot share with one another," he said, his fingers savoring the satin softness of her skin. A near painful ache clenched his stomach. Not just the all too familiar pang of desire, he acknowledged as he gazed deeply into her wide eyes, but a lingering wound of loneliness far more potent than mere lust. He had missed being with this woman. Missed teasing her and seeing the flash of her eyes and the smelling the scent of her skin. "Victoria . . ." he breathed.

As if sensing the sudden shift in the atmosphere, she regarded him warily. "Yes?"

"I have longed to kiss you," he said simply.

There was a startled silence as she gave a faint tremble. "Oh."

Encouraged that she had not instantly retreated from his advance, Claredon cupped her chin with gentle fingers. "May I hold you in my arms?"

He knew he was taking a risk by leaving the choice open to her. It would have been far easier to simply

sweep her into his arms and make love to her until
she could no longer tell him no. Without arrogance,
he knew he could seduce this stubborn woman. But
he had made his decision. He wanted her to come to
him freely, without regrets.

Her breath quickened, and Claredon feared that
he had gambled and lost. Then, with a sweet hesi-
tancy, she gave a nod of her head. "Yes."

Perhaps absurdly, Claredon felt as nervous as a
schoolboy as he removed her bonnet and tenderly
wrapped his arms about her to pull her close to the
hardness of his frame. He gave a low groan as her
soft curves pressed to his body, her hair tickling his
nose in a delicious manner. That ache within became
a pulsing need that made his knees tremble.

"You feel so perfect," he muttered, burying his
face in her fiery curls. "As if you were made to fit
against me."

She shivered as his hands moved urgently down
her spine, gently pressing her closer to his tightened
thighs. "Perhaps you were made to fit against me,"
she teased in a satisfyingly breathless voice.

He closed his eyes to allow the sheer joy of holding
her close to rush through him. "I can think of no better reason to be born."

Almost tentatively, her hands lifted to lie against
the width of his chest. Claredon caught his breath
at her innocent caress.

"Claredon . . ." she whispered in low tones.

"Yes, my love?"

Her head tilted back to regard him with dark, be-
mused eyes. "I . . ."

"Tell me, Victoria," he urged, feeling as if he were
standing on a precipice that might very well destroy
him if he took a misstep. "What do you want?"

She gave a slow shake of her head. "I do not know."

Realizing she was simply too shy to put into words the sensations that were making her shiver with longing, Claredon carefully swept her into his arms and, tossing aside the Holland cover upon the sofa, gently laid her upon the cushions.

Looking down upon her vulnerable expression, he felt his heart turn over in his chest. She looked so utterly sweet with her hair billowed about her pale countenance and her eyes dark with desire. He so desperately wanted to please her. Not only in a physical sense, but as her husband. To become the man she could one day love.

"Victoria," he breathed in low tones. "I desire you very much, but I will not pressure you to offer more than you are prepared to give." He paused as he searched her face. "Do you trust me?"

Slowly, astonishingly, she lifted her arms in welcome. "Yes, Claredon. I trust you."

Twelve

Victoria felt . . . what?

Alive, certainly.

Fulfilled.

Utterly safe.

And oddly smug.

Lying in the circle of Claredon's arms, Victoria snuggled close to his warmth. She had expected to enjoy the pleasure of her husband's possession. Despite her refusal to give in to temptation, she had known deep within her that she desired Claredon. And the mere fact that she had far too often dreamed of this precise moment revealed her inner wish to discover the full wonder of his lovemaking.

What she hadn't expected was the sheer intensity of the sensations that had rushed through her, or the ready manner in which Claredon revealed his own potent need. More than once, he had lost his famed expertise and fumbled in haste, making her feel beautiful and sinfully sensuous. She had opened herself, making herself wholly vulnerable, but the knowledge that Claredon had done the same gave her a sense of power she had never thought to experience.

A shiver raced through her as Claredon stroked his lips over the tender skin of her temple. "This was not how I intended this to be," he murmured with rueful humor.

Feeling more confident than she had in her entire life, Victoria turned her head to meet his narrowed gaze. "You have regrets?"

His arms abruptly tightened about her slender form. "Dear lord, no. How could I regret the most precious thing that has ever occurred in my life? But I had thought to make our first time together somewhat more romantic."

Victoria was utterly glad that it had not been a planned seduction. The swift, uncontrollable passion that had spiraled between them had been far more exciting, more genuine than a practiced assault upon her senses. "I suppose there is something rather romantic about a hidden cottage," she assured him.

He gave a rather wicked smile. "I will admit that it is far more romantic now than it was as a child. Pretending to be a pirate or a knight was never so pleasurable."

Breathing in deeply of the warm male scent of him, she smiled archly. "Of course, you did rather deceive me."

Without warning he stiffened, as if fearing that she were about to accuse him of something dreadful. "Indeed?"

"You said that you never seduced women here," she reminded him softly.

He breathed out a soft sigh, his hand running down the length of her back. "Never before today, and I do not care for the word seduced," he chastised. "It implies I stole from you what you were not entirely willing to give."

Her skin tingled at the warmth of his fingers

traced a delicate pattern over the curve of her hip. "You know that is not true," she said with a faint blush.

"I sincerely hope it is not." He shifted so that he could lean upon his elbow and gaze into her face with a suddenly somber expression. "You asked if I had regrets. Now I ask you the same."

Although still shy at discussing what had just occurred between them, Victoria resisted the urge to give a flippant response. She sensed that her answer was important to Claredon. "No," she said simply.

"Thank God." His eyes briefly closed before he opened them to smile deep into her gaze. Obviously her answer was even more important than she had suspected. "I do not think I could bear . . . gads, Victoria, you make me feel as uncertain as a schoolboy."

She regarded him in shock. Could this be the arrogant, consummate master of women she had wed? Suddenly he seemed as bewildered by the emotions that had surged between them as she was. It was as endearing as it was unexpected, and Victoria's heart glowed with a perilous joy.

"You?" she at last forced herself to tease in light tones, not entirely certain she wished to feel so dangerously entangled with this man.

His lips twitched at her exaggerated shock. "Do you find that amusing, my minx?"

"I find it unbelievable," she retorted in all honesty. "You are far too arrogant and assured of your own charms to ever feel uncertain."

He gave a slow shake of his head, his hand pulling her abruptly against his body. "Only when it did not matter," he said in dark tones. "And this does matter, Victoria. It matters a great deal."

The very world seemed to halt as she gazed into

his darkened blue eyes. It *was* important, she suddenly realized. Perhaps the most important thing in her entire life.

"Yes," she breathed.

For long moments they gazed at one another, both searching for the unspoken questions that still lay between them. Where did they go from here? How had their relationship changed? Had the regret and anger that had marred their marriage been at long last laid to rest?

At last, a cloud scuttling across the sun, leaving the late afternoon in shadows, prompted Claredon to give a faint sigh. "As much as I would like to remain here an eternity, I suppose we should consider inspecting the land and returning home. I would not wish Mr. Humbly to worry over our absence."

He was right, of course. The poor vicar had been fretting and worrying over them since Mr. Smith had first made his appearance. She would not wish him to become concerned.

Still, she discovered herself reluctant to rise. However absurd it might be after what had just passed between them, she could not blithely parade about naked before Claredon.

"I . . ."

Her husband frowned at her hesitation. "What is it, Victoria?"

Feeling every sort of a fool, she pressed her heated face into his shoulder. "Would you turn your back while I attire myself?"

"What?" he demanded in surprise.

"I know it is ridiculous, but . . ."

"No," he abruptly interrupted, reaching up to cup her chin and force her to meet his tender gaze. "You are bound to be shy for a time. Just hold on a moment." With the elegant grace that was so much a part of him, Claredon rose to his feet. Then, with swift movements, he gathered the Holland cover from the floor and held it up like a curtain between them. "Now you can have your privacy."

Deeply relieved that he had not mocked her childish embarrassment, Victoria reached for the garments that had been scattered across the floor. In moments she had managed to slip on her shift and stockings, but after pulling on her habit, she reluctantly realized there was no possibility of reaching the hooks and buttons that fastened the garment in the back.

"Blast," she muttered in exasperation. She had not considered the realization she would need a maid to help her after such an interlude. How did other women manage?

"Is there a problem?" he asked in faintly amused tones.

She bit her lip, knowing that she had no choice but to confess her dilemma. "I cannot button my habit."

Without warning, the Holland cover dropped to the floor, and he regarded her with a wicked smile.

"Ah, that is because it is a task for your husband. Allow me."

Unlike her, Claredon did not appear to possess the least shred of modesty as he stepped toward her. Smothering a nervous giggle, she abruptly turned so he could reach the buttons.

With considerably more skill than he had exhibited in removing her habit, Claredon set about refastening the hooks and tiny buttons. He had managed to reach the middle of her back when, without warning, he abruptly leaned downward to press warm lips to her bare skin.

Victoria gave a violent jump at the shocking pleasure that raced through her. "Claredon," she
protested in uneven tones, "you are supposed to be
fastening the buttons."

He gave a low groan. "I have discovered I far prefer undoing them."

Much to her astonishment, Victoria could feel the
tempting heat begin to swirl through her lower stomach once again. She had not dreamed that a woman
could experience desire so rapidly.

"You said that we must go," she said, more to keep
herself from melting to her knees than from any true
urge to leave their private cottage.

"Perhaps I spoke too hastily," he murmured, his
lips tracing a silky path up her spine to the base of
her neck. "If Mr. Humbly is visiting the rector, then
it might be several hours before he misses us."

Against her will, Victoria's head fell backward as
the persuasive delight of his caress sizzled to the very
tip of her toes. She felt nearly overwhelmed by the
force of her need, and more than a little frightened.
It had been difficult enough to remain impervious
to his charm before she had allowed such intimacies.
How could she possibly resist now? "I think it best we
return," she muttered cowardly.

"The voice of reason," he sighed, allowing himself one last kiss before finishing his task. She heard
a rustle as he gathered his own clothes and set about
restoring his usual elegance. "You can turn about
now. I am decent."

Slowly turning, she discovered him slipping on his
jacket and smoothing the thick curls from his face.
He looked unbearably handsome, even when he
gave a rueful grimace at his crumpled cravat and
tossed it onto the sofa. His arrogant features were

softened and almost boyish as he held out an arm to lead her from the cottage.

With a tiny thrill at the knowledge this wonderful, enticing gentleman was truly her husband now, Victoria readily stepped forward to lay her hand upon his offered arm. Together they stepped into the sunshine, pulling the door closed behind them. She moved toward the waiting ladder, only to be halted as Claredon suddenly grasped her shoulders and turned her to face him.

"What is it?" she demanded as he simply gazed at her with a searching gaze.

"I did not . . . hurt you?"

It took a moment for her to realize he was referring to the loss of her innocence. A revealing warmth rose beneath her cheeks. "I am fine," she assured him.

"You must tell me if you are sore, or in any way discomforted. I would never wish to cause you pain," he persisted, somehow knowing that she was indeed tender from their intimacy. "You promise me?"

It had been far too long since anyone had shown such unwavering concern for her welfare. Victoria felt ridiculous tears prick at her eyes. It was rather a wonderful thing to have someone care for her. "Yes."

He smiled tenderly, brushing one of her stray curls from her cheek. "Are you ready?"

"Certainly."

"Have a care," he warned as he held the ladder steady and watched her make her way to the ground. He was swift to follow behind, placing her hand back on his arm as he turned her toward the pathway.

"What of the ladder?" she demanded as they moved through the undergrowth.

He smiled as he tugged her closer. "I believe I shall

leave it down. I possess great hopes you shall wish to return in the very near future."

With a stealth that would have made the finest criminal proud, Claredon slipped through the still sleeping household and into his wife's bedchamber. A thoroughly ridiculous smile curved his lips as he moved across the carpet toward the large canopy bed.

It had been only a few hours since he had covertly slipped from this room after making slow, delicious love to Victoria. He had wanted nothing more than to remain wrapped in her arms through the rest of the night, but he had sensed her innocent embarrassment at the thought of having the servants discover him in her bed.

He could not deny a small part of him rued her shyness. He wanted to shout to the world that this amazing woman was now his in the most intimate way possible. He wanted to claim her in the possessive manner of any male. And yet, he found her innocence enchanting.

He was a gentleman accustomed to experienced women who sought their pleasure with practiced ease, women who desired his company for one purpose only. In contrast, Victoria had been awkward, untutored, and utterly delightful. Her responses had not come from skill, but from the heart.

She was not a woman who could ever separate the two.

That knowledge had sent a chill of fear down his spine. It would be bad enough to disappoint a lover. To disappoint the woman who had reluctantly offered him a piece of her heart would be unbearable. Then he had gathered his wits.

He would not disappoint Victoria. He would do everything possible to be the husband she desired.

With that thought firmly in mind, he had left his bed at an ungodly hour to make his way to the conservatory, and now was slipping into his wife's bedroom like a lovesick moonling.

Perching upon the edge of the bed, he allowed himself a moment to study her in early morning light.

A smile curved his lips at the splash of vibrant red curls artlessly spread across the pillow and the thick black crescent of her lashes, which lay against her cheek. She looked as fragile and untouched as the newly bloomed rose he held in his fingers.

Leaning forward, he lightly brushed the flower beneath her nose. The potent musk filled the air, and with a small sigh she rolled onto her back. With a low chuckle, he once again waved the satin petals beneath her nose and watched as her lashes fluttered upward.

"Good morning, my dear," he whispered.

Her emerald eyes were still clouded with lingering sleep as she regarded him with a faint frown. "Claredon?"

With a flourish, he held out the rose for her. "A present for you."

Her breath caught as she reached out to take the proffered flower with understanding. "A rose."

"I wished to prove that I can be as romantic as the next gentleman upon occasion."

Pushing herself to a sitting position, she demurely kept the covers about her slender frame as she offered him a tentative smile. "That is very kind."

His own smile was wicked. "No, it is very selfish."

"Selfish?"

"I desired an excuse to visit my wife at this unreasonable hour," he said, delighted when she raised a flustered hand to her tangle of curls.

"I cannot think why. I must be a mess."

He gave a slow shake of his head. Even with her hair mussed and her countenance flushed with sleep, he had never seen a more achingly beautiful sight. "You are adorable, as you always are," he assured her.

A sudden twinkle of amusement entered her emerald eyes. "That is a bald-faced lie, sir."

Quite willing to prove how adorable he found her to be, he leaned forward. "Shall I demonstrate just how adorable I find you, my minx?"

She sank into the pillows with a shy hint of excitement glowing in her eyes. "Claredon, my maid will be here soon."

He reached out to softly outline her lips with the tip of his finger. A wave of satisfaction raced through him as they readily parted at his touch. "We could always lock the door."

Sweet anticipation rippled over her features, warming his heart and other places in his body before she glanced anxiously toward the door. He could imagine her picturing the knowing glint in her maid's eyes when she came with the morning chocolate only to find the door locked against her.

"I . . ." she began, only to be silenced as he gently pressed his fingers to her mouth.

"No, you are not yet comfortable."

She smiled with relief at his understanding. "I suppose you think I am being childish."

His expression became somber as he regarded the woman who had become such a vital part of his life. "Victoria, this is all very new to you, and I happen to find your shyness quite enchanting. I wish only to please you. I want you to be happy in this marriage."

She absorbed his words in silence. Then she regarded him with a searching gaze. "And what do you want, Claredon?"

He raised startled brows at her unexpected question. "Besides you?"

She blushed. "Yes."

Claredon gave himself time to ponder the question. He had spent five months saying precisely the wrong thing to this woman. For once he wanted to get it right. "You know, for a very long time I thought I desired an impossible fantasy. A woman who could not possibly exist."

Her eyes darkened with regret. "And now you will never discover her."

He gave a shake of his head, his finger moving beneath her chin to keep her gaze firmly entangled with her own. "I had already discovered her," he said in firm tones. "Only I was too blind and too angry at being forced into marriage to realize the truth."

Her expression became wary, as if she feared that he might be mocking her. "You have discovered her?"

"Oh, yes." He smiled with warm tenderness. "And she is everything I have ever hoped she would be. Intelligent, beautiful, tender of heart, yet with an independent spirit. And best of all, she possesses the most amazing ability to please her husband."

"I thought I was a sharp-tongued shrew," she retorted in uncertain tones.

Claredon gave a rich chuckle, his entire being filled with a shimmering happiness. He could not name this strange, unfathomable emotion that made his head dizzy and his heart swell with joy, but he was not about to fight it. "Only when you feel the need to protect yourself. Just as I attempted to provoke you to keep a distance between us."

A fragile glow of hope entered her emerald eyes as she searched his relaxed countenance. "We were both rather foolish."

He gave a faint shrug, no longer willing to dwell upon the past. It was his future with this woman that he wished to consider. "Yes, but perhaps we needed time to become accustomed to our situation. It would have been impossible to have been thrown into marriage without a few misunderstandings."

"Yes," she slowly agreed.

His hand moved to stroke the tempting line of her neck, and he was amazed, as always, by the perfect silk of her skin. "The wait certainly wetted my appetite," he murmured with a meaningful smile.

She gave a breathy laugh, her eyes suddenly dark with the delicious knowledge of her power over him. "You are shameless," she chided, but her voice held no sting.

"Only with you, Victoria." He gazed deep into those bewitching eyes. "I meant what I said. You are my wife, and I will be faithful to you."

Her gaze did not waver as she reached out to lightly touch his cheek with the tips of her fingers. "I trust you."

They were the most beautiful words he had ever heard, and it took every shred of willpower he possessed not to cover her with his body and prove to her just how deeply she had moved him.

"You are certain you would not like to lock the door?" he said in a rasping voice.

She briefly wavered as a shiver shook her body, but she gave a faint shake of her head. "Not yet."

"Very well," he agreed without rancor. Someday she would be ready to forget the world for the pleasure of love. He could be patient. "What will you do today?"

She gave a reluctant grimace. "I suppose I should be a proper hostess, since we abandoned our guest yesterday."

Claredon grimly refused to allow any thought of Thomas Stice to mar his goodwill. Victoria had already admitted that she had never loved the fool. And if she still cared for him as a friend, he was surely a big enough man to accept their relationship.

Well, perhaps not accept, he ruefully acknowledged. He still longed to blacken the nitwit's eye and toss him from the estate. But he was at least wise enough not to reveal his utterly male desire to keep his woman from the company of another gentleman. "Very proper," he managed to murmur in reasonably neutral tones.

"And what of you?" she demanded.

"I believe I shall call upon Lord Vernon and make an offer for his land," Claredon abruptly decided, knowing better than to press his dubious control by watching Mr. Stice cling to his wife in his cowardly fashion. "If we have more than one son, we shall need estates to leave to them."

Her eyes widened at his casual reference to their future children. Then a fiercely pleased glow entered her eyes. It was obvious she had not considered the thought of the inevitable conclusion to their new intimacy. Thankfully, the thought seemed to please her rather than shock her.

"What if we have only daughters?" she teased.

He shrugged, not at all put out by the thought. He had enough cousins to ensure the line would continue whatever the sex of his children. "Then the land we purchase will remain unentailed so they can inherit. I do not doubt our daughters will be just as capable as their mother of running an estate."

He had hoped to reassure her with his determined words, but without warning, her eyes suddenly filled with tears. "Oh."

Horrified at the thought of unintentionally wounding her, Claredon scooted close to her and cupped her face between his hands. "Dear heavens, what is it, Victoria?"

Gazing at him with tear-drenched eyes, she gave a small hiccup. "I believe that is the nicest thing you have ever said to me."

Amazement battled with surging relief as he gave a choked laugh. Gads, but she had frightened him. He did not ever want to see her cry. "Oh, my dear, only you would be more pleased to be admired for your management skills than to be likened to an angel," he said ruefully.

Blithely unaware that she had momentarily terrified him she sent him, a stern frown. "You will not go to Lord Vernon's alone?" she commanded.

"No, I will take Peter with me," he readily agreed, not about to take chances with his life now that he had so much to live for.

"And you will not take foolish risks?" she persisted.

Leaning down, he feathered a kiss over her tempting lips. "I promise you nothing will keep me from your bed tonight," he husked. With a great deal of reluctance, he rose to his feet. Blast, but he wanted to stay—for an eternity. "Now I suppose I should go before that wretched maid makes her appearance. Until later, my love."

Her smile held all the promise of paradise. "Until later."

Thirteen

An hour later, Victoria was aimlessly sketching the roses in the conservatory.

Despite her earlier determination to devote herself to her guests, she had discovered herself unable to force her reluctant feet to carry her to the breakfast room. Instead she had silently slipped through the halls with a secretive smile and the need to be alone with her thoughts.

How could she possibly chatter aimlessly with Mr. Humbly? Or listen to Thomas's endless moaning when all she desired to do was dance about the house, singing at the top of her voice?

Her eyes slid closed as she allowed the pleasurable memories to rush through her.

Yesterday in the cottage, Claredon had revealed a tender care that had touched her very soul. Last night . . .

Ah, last night he had revealed a fiery need that had made her feel utterly desired. She shivered as delicious sensations raced through her.

Never in her wildest dreams had she thought she could be so wanton, so abandoned, or that her ready response could be so provocative for her husband.

The very fact that she had even managed to shock herself had made her reluctant to allow others to realize that they were now truly man and wife. It was absurd, she knew. But she could not seem to toss aside years of modesty in just a few hours.

A rather wicked smile curved her lips.

Besides, it was decidedly lovely to have her husband sneaking into her room to awaken her with a rose.

Her heart gave that dangerous quiver, but, with an unconscious toss of her head, she shoved aside the knowledge she was treading in dangerous waters. Perhaps her emotions were becoming hopelessly tangled, but she could no longer conjure up the barriers she had once kept between herself and Claredon.

The sound of the door to the conservatory opening had her turning about to discover Mr. Humbly walking down the pathway toward her. With an effort, she attempted to disguise the giddy smile she was certain would give her away.

"There you are, my dear," he murmured as he settled upon the small bench beside her.

"Mr. Humbly."

He leaned forward to peer at the sketch she had started of the nearby roses. "How very lovely."

"Thank you."

He watched her set aside the sketch with a faint smile. "We missed you at breakfast."

A stab of guilt assaulted her at the realization that she had been a poor hostess for this kindly gentleman. Not only had he been shaken out of his wits by a thief, but she had brutally condemned him to hours alone with Thomas. No doubt he would have preferred the thief.

"Forgive me," she murmured with genuine regret. "But I awoke this morning with the urge to make a few sketches."

"And no wonder, you are very talented," he replied, without the least hint of censure.

His sweet nature only made her feel even more guilty, and she gave a rueful grimace. "Oh, no, I merely dabble. Addy was always the true artist," she said, referring to her dear friend from Surrey.

Humbly gave a nod of his head. "She is most remarkable. She recently painted my portrait, you know."

"Did she?"

"It was quite good," he commended with a sudden twinkle in his eyes. "Although Mrs. Stalwart was terribly disappointed that Addy managed to capture me so accurately."

Victoria lifted her brows. "Surely that is the purpose of a portrait."

Humbly grimaced. "I believe she thought it would be more dignified if I had been given more hair and fewer chins."

"Nonsense," Victoria loyally denied. This gentleman was perhaps the most gentle, kindly person she had ever had the pleasure of meeting. She wouldn't change a hair or chin. "You are perfect as you are."

He chuckled at her fierce tone. "That is very kind of you, my dear."

"How is Addy?" she demanded, suddenly realizing just how much she missed the companionship of her childhood friends. Addy could always make her laugh, while her other friend, Beatrice, was the more sensible of their group. Together they had forged unshakable bonds that would last a lifetime.

"Very happy, I am pleased to say," the vicar replied promptly.

"I am relieved." She gave a small frown. "She was

not wholly enamored of the thought of wedding Mr. Drake."

Humbly gave a vague lift of his hands. "As with all new marriages, there were a few difficulties in becoming accustomed to one another. Both Addy and Adam possessed expectations of one another that interfered with realizing the truth of their feelings. Once they took the time to seek an understanding, all was well."

Victoria knew all too well the difficulties of being newly married. Gads, her own wedding had been a hurried affair followed by months of brittle anger. It would be a pleasure to put such days behind her.

"I am very happy for her."

"As am I," Humbly said with a smile. "And I am pleased to say that Beatrice is doing quite well."

"I did not doubt that she would be very pleased with her marriage," Victoria retorted, recalling her friend's near delirious pleasure at having discovered the gentleman of her dreams. "She loved Lord Faulconer very much."

Humbly gave a sad shake of his head. "Yes, until she discovered that he was in dire need of her inheritance."

Victoria regarded him in shock. Her gentle, shy Beatrice had been duped by a scoundrel? A fierce wave of anger raced through her. "He was a fortune hunter?" she gritted.

"I believe that was the reason he sought an introduction to Beatrice."

Victoria clenched her hands in her lap. To think she had even liked Lord Faulconer. He had seemed so devoted to Beatrice. "Why the . . . lout," she breathed.

"Do not be too harsh," Humbly said in gentle tones. "He is a very fine gentleman and loves Beatrice to distraction. Besides, I believe he was suitably punished for his initial deception."

"I should hope so," she said, not entirely forgiving the man who had hurt her friend.

"Thankfully, they have worked through their troubles, and Beatrice found it within her heart to forgive her husband." He regarded her in a knowing manner. "Not an easy task, but one that has brought her peace. It is not pleasant to live with anger and bitterness."

Realizing he was no longer referring to Beatrice, but to her own relationship with Claredon, Victoria smiled wryly. "Yes, I know."

There was a brief silence as he studied her delicate countenance. "How are you, Victoria? You were very quiet at dinner last evening."

Despite all her determination to maintain her composure, Victoria could not halt the faint blush that rose to her cheeks. She had barely been able to swallow a morsel during dinner last evening, with her husband sending her those smoldering glances that promised delicious pleasure soon to come. It was a wonder that the dining room table had not been consumed in flames by the heat in his eyes. "I am well."

His brow wrinkled at her choked tone. "Is anything troubling you?"

Knowing that the gentleman was far too wise to be put off for long, she flashed him a dry smile. "Do you mean besides a madman stalking me and an ex-fiancé as a houseguest?"

Thankfully put off the track, the vicar gave a low chuckle. "Troubles, indeed."

"It will all pass," she said with a shrug.

Humbly tilted his head to one side. "Well, there is little I can do to help with the madman, but I would be quite willing to keep Mr. Stice occupied until he leaves."

Caught off guard by the generous offer, Victoria gave an instinctive shake of her head. "Oh, no, I could not ask that of you."

He merely smiled. "I do not mind."

"That is because you do not fully comprehend what you are offering," she said before she could halt the impulsive words.

Humbly gave a cough, a twinkle in his sherry eyes. "I have discovered that Mr. Stice can be somewhat . . . smothering."

She grimaced at the hours she had been forced to endure Thomas's self-pity. "That is a polite means of describing him."

Too late she realized that she was revealing far more than she had intended. Humbly gave a lift of his brow as he studied her with a narrowed gaze. "May I presume you are no longer so disappointed that your elopement with Mr. Stice was halted?"

Her gaze dropped to hide her sheer horror at the thought of being trapped with Thomas for the next fifty years. Dear heavens, she would have been miserable within the first week.

"I cannot deny that I had been foolishly impulsive," she admitted in cautious tones. "I did not know Thomas nearly well enough to have contemplated marriage."

With his usual kindness, Humbly reached out to cover her hand with his own. "It is not so surprising, Victoria. You are a woman with a great need to reach out and help others. It is quite simple to mistake pity for love."

It was what she had told herself, but a lingering sense of fear remained lodged deep in her heart, a fear she could not possibly speak of with Claredon. "That is truly not a comfort, Mr. Humbly," she said in wry tones.

Perhaps sensing her inner vulnerability, Humbly leaned forward to regard her with an encouraging smile. "What is it, Victoria?"

She paused for a long moment before giving a restless shrug. "If I could be so mistaken in my feelings once, how can I trust them again?" she questioned in low tones.

His hand tightened upon her fingers as his expression became somber. "There are no certainties in life, Victoria, and it can be frightening to make yourself vulnerable to another."

A faint tremor raced through her body. She had already made herself more vulnerable to Claredon than she had ever dreamed possible, and at the same time exposed her heart to disappointment.

She might have learned to trust Claredon, but he had never offered her more than his passion. How could she possibly give of her heart if he could never return her emotions? Surely it would be unbearable to fall in love with a man who would never love her, who might even be discomforted by the burden of her attachment. "Yes," she breathed softly.

He gave her hand a last pat before he sat back and offered her a reassuring smile. "All I do know is that love should be about two people placing the other's happiness above their own, not one person taking and the other always giving."

Her features abruptly softened. "That is what my parents possessed."

"And what you will one day possess, Victoria. Of that I am certain." Raising himself to his feet, Humbly folded his hands across his protruding stomach. "Now

I believe I shall go in search of Mr. Stice. Enjoy your morning, my dear."

Nearly two hours later, Victoria went in search of her husband. She knew it was ridiculous, but she felt distinctly uneasy at the thought of him galloping across the countryside, even with a groom at his side. She would not be at ease until he returned safely.

Knowing he would more than likely seek his library once he reached Longmeade, she briskly made her way through the house and entered the book-lined room. It came as a decided shock to discover Thomas already there, standing beside the desk and frowning down at a piece of paper in his hand.

Cowardly considering slipping out before she was noticed, Victoria was halted as Thomas abruptly lifted his head and regarded her in surprise.

More or less trapped, she forced a stiff smile to her lips. "Oh, Thomas, good morning."

"Good morning, Victoria," he murmured, although his gaze strayed back to the paper.

Curious at his odd distraction, she put aside her reluctance to spend a moment longer in his company than necessary and crossed the room. "Is something the matter?"

"It is the oddest thing."

"What is?"

He glanced upward at her approach and waved a vague hand toward the nearby desk. "I was searching for wax to seal my letter to Mother when I happened across this sketch of Andrew. I did not realize that the two of you were acquainted."

Sketch?

Victoria's breath froze in her throat as she moved

to view the paper he held in his hand. Dear heavens, it was the sketch she had drawn of the villain, she acknowledged in dazed disbelief.

Licking her dry lips, she studied Thomas's baffled expression. "Andrew?"

"Yes. Andrew Banfield, my cousin," he readily responded, unaware of her sudden tension. "Is this not him?"

With hands that suddenly shook, Victoria took the sketch from his grasp. "I made this sketch from a description of a thief who attempted to sneak into our library window."

"What?" Thomas frowned in disbelief at her implication. "That is impossible."

Realizing that it would be unwise to leap to conclusions, Victoria attempted to calm her racing heart. Thomas could very well be mistaken. It was, after all, only the merest sketch made from the fuddled memories of Mr. Humbly.

"Tell me of your cousin. You never mentioned him before."

Thomas gave a shrug, regarding her as if he feared she might be a tad noddy. "I fear that Mother does not truly approve of him."

Victoria swallowed a smile. Mrs. Stice did not approve of anyone who could not be used to further her aspirations in Society. "Why not?"

He waved a dismissive hand. "You know Mother. She did not approve of his gambling or his habit of consorting with actresses."

It was certainly not much to go upon, but Victoria did at least know that Andrew was a gambling man, the sort of man who might easily be in need of quick profits. "And now your mother's jewels are missing," she muttered, beginning to believe Claredon's insistence that this could not all be a coincidence.

"Yes . . ." Thomas suddenly appeared thunderstruck. "I say, Victoria, you cannot mean to imply that Andrew stole the jewels?"

She knew it must sound absurd. What proof did she have? Nothing more than a vague sketch and a vague intuition.

"It is the only thing that makes sense," she retorted, as much to convince herself as her companion. "But why would he believe that I now possess them?"

Thomas gave a petulant pout, clearly not desiring to discuss such an unpleasant subject. He far preferred to turn his head from such matters and let others deal with them. "I haven't the faintest notion what you are speaking about," he complained.

She thinned her lips with irritation, not about to allow him to avoid her questions. It was too important to worry over sensitive nerves. "When was the last time you saw your cousin?"

He gave a restless shrug, shifting his feet as if considering bolting from the room. "I do not know. Perhaps three weeks ago."

"Did he mention anything of your mother's jewels?"

"Of course not," he huffed, thoroughly out of charity with her probing questions. "Andrew knew nothing of Mother's missing jewels. Indeed, he spoke only of his ill luck at the tables and . . ." He stammered to a sudden halt, his brow furrowed as he recalled his conversation with his cousin.

"What is it?" she demanded in sharp tones.

"Well, he did seem particularly interested in the figurine I had purchased for you. He said he wished to have it duplicated for a gift to his latest mistress," he admitted slowly. "He seemed rather put out when

I said I had already sent it to you as an engagement gift. I thought it odd at the time. Andrew has always assured me that my taste is horrible. Take this coat, for instance . . ."

"Thomas," she firmly interrupted, not about to become distracted. "You are certain he was interested in the figurine you sent to me?"

Thomas gave a shrug. "I suppose it caught his fancy when I showed it to him earlier that week."

Figurine?

It made no sense. Although she had not examined the gift closely, she was certain it was not worth stealing. It was indeed a rather ugly figure of a woman attired in one of the wide gowns preferred years ago. There were no jewels or . . .

Suddenly she was struck with inspiration.

Perhaps there were jewels—only she had not yet discovered them.

Grasping Thomas's arm, she tugged him impatiently toward the door. "Come along."

"Victoria, where are we going?" he demanded, stumbling over his feet as she hustled him across the carpet and into the hall.

"I will show you," she promised, not slowing her pace as she moved up the stairs and down the upper hallway. Reaching her chambers, she threw open the door and hurried inside.

"Good heavens, Victoria," Thomas said as he stubbornly halted just outside the door.

"What is it?"

"I cannot enter your bedchamber."

"Oh for goodness sakes," she muttered, leaving him behind to move toward the tiny table beside her bed where she had placed the figurine. Grasping it, she hurried back to where Thomas waited. "Here it is."

"The figurine?" Thomas demanded in surprise.

"There must be something . . ." she muttered, studying the figurine with a searching gaze. At last she turned it over to discover that in the back of the gown was a small latch. With trembling fingers, she tugged it upward to discover a clever door cut in the porcelain. It was obviously designed to hold a woman's personal belongings, she realized with a leap of her heart. It was also obvious that someone else's belongings were already tucked inside. "Oh!"

"What is it?" Thomas demanded.

Barely able to make her shaking fingers work properly, Victoria tipped the figurine so that the gaudy diamond necklace and matching earrings tumbled into her open palm.

"Look," she breathed.

"Mother's jewels," Thomas exclaimed in shock. "But how did they get into the figurine?"

Not quite believing that her wild suspicions were now indeed confirmed, she gave a slow shake of her head. "I would say that only Andrew could answer that question."

Thomas abruptly stepped backward, his brow creased with a fierce scowl. "No, it is not possible. Andrew would never be involved in such an unsavory thing."

Not about to waste time arguing with the ridiculous man, Victoria swept past him and headed down the stairs.

"I must find Claredon," she said, nearly trembling with the need to find her husband and reveal what she had discovered.

"Victoria, wait . . ." Thomas called from behind her.

Victoria did not even bother to turn about as she flew over the steps and through the lower hall.

Her only thought was finding her husband. He would comprehend the importance of her discovery. More importantly, he would know precisely what was to be done. He was a man she could depend upon utterly, she realized with a vague stab of surprise, not quite certain when she had begun to lean upon him for support. It could not just be since she had given herself to him in a physical sense. She must have known all along that he was a gentleman of strength, despite her determination to keep him a distance.

It was rather a disquieting realization.

Shaking her head at the absurdity of her thoughts, she moved through the hallway, desperately hoping that Claredon had returned.

She saw no sight of him until she at last reached the foyer, where the young groom was just entering. "Oh, Peter, I am so glad you have returned," she exclaimed as she hurried toward him. "Do you know where I can find Lord Claredon?"

Astonishingly, the servant gave a low moan as he wrung his hands together. "My lady, he has been taken."

Too shocked to fully comprehend his agonized words, Victoria regarded him in blank confusion. "Taken? What do you mean?"

"We were riding through the woods when a masked rider appeared with a gun."

Pain that nearly sent her to her knees sliced through Victoria as she reached out to clutch onto a heavy side table. No, it could not be possible. Claredon had promised to take care. He had promised he would return to their bed that night.

"Dear lord, he isn't . . ." She could not even bear to utter the gut-wrenching words, afraid that speaking of her terror would make it true.

"He is well," the servant was swift to assure her, "but the bugger . . . beg pardon, the scoundrel forced him to go with him. He said that the jewels and a thousand pounds were to be left by three this afternoon at the precise spot where he abducted his lordship."

Only sheer effort kept Victoria from swooning in relief. Claredon was alive. At the moment that was the only thing that mattered.

Several minutes passed as she struggled to regain her wits enough to contemplate what was to be done. She had to be strong, she sternly reprimanded herself. Later she could have her hysterics. For now, her only thought must be for saving Claredon before it was too late.

"We must organize a search," she at last managed to command in surprisingly steady tones. "And I must send for the magistrate . . ."

"My lady," Peter abruptly intruded into her thoughts.

She offered him an impatient frown. "What?"

"He said that you were to come alone or he . . ." The young man's voice abruptly broke.

Victoria's blood ran cold. "Or what?"

"Or he would kill his lordship."

Fourteen

Victoria hovered on the edge of panic.

Dear heavens, what had she done? Pacing the length of the library, she battled the tears of fear and frustration that threatened to overwhelm her. Why had she listened to Humbly and the others?

Her only concern was ensuring her husband was brought home safely. But rather than heeding the whispers of her heart, she had allowed herself to be swayed by the arguments of the vicar and the servants.

They had urged her not to give in to the demands to leave the jewels and money in the clearing as had been ordered.

Humbly had worried that once the villain had what he desired, he would put a swift end to Claredon. After all, Andrew Banfield did not yet realize that they had discovered his identity. To his mind, only Claredon could finger him for the crime. It would be foolish to leave behind a witness.

They had insisted that she allow the servants to position themselves throughout the woods so that the thief could be caught when he came for his bounty. That way, they could follow him back to his hideout and save Claredon from a certain death.

So while she had desperately searched the house

to discover the necessary funds, Humbly had organized a covert means of slipping the servants from the house to the outlying buildings and eventually to a variety of hidden locations throughout the woods. He had insisted each servant leave at least a half an hour apart so that no one watching the house would be suspicious.

At precisely a quarter till three, Victoria had taken a small bag filled with the jewels and money to the location that Peter had described. She had left the small fortune behind and returned to the house to await word of the thief's capture. It was not until nearly dark that Humbly had given up hope, retrieved the bag, and returned to the house with the servants.

Now she and Humbly paced through the library with no notion of what was to be done next.

"I knew that I should have just left the jewels and money." She at last broke the thick silence, her heart twisting with a sick dread. "Dear God, what if Claredon is already injured?"

Humbly swiftly crossed to her, his expression set in grim lines. "No, Victoria, this gentleman is clearly determined to collect a fortune. He will be far more dangerous once he has what he desires. Until then, he must keep Lord Claredon safe."

She twined her fingers together, wishing she possessed the vicar's faith. "But now we do not even know what we are to do."

"The scoundrel will no doubt send a message of some sort," Humbly comforted. "And if he follows true to form, he will be adding another thousand pounds in the bargain."

Victoria waved a dismissive hand. She did not care if he asked for the deed to Longmeade. She would give up everything she possessed to have Claredon home safely. She would give up her own life, if necessary.

Her eyes slipped closed as she battled the rise of hysterics. Until she had been forced to consider the thought of losing Claredon, she had not realized just how vital he had become to her life. So vital she was not at all certain she could go on without him. "I do not care what he asks for, as long as Claredon is safe."

As if sensing how near she was to a complete collapse, Humbly reached out to kindly pat her arm. "All will be well, my dear."

Tears flooded her eyes, despite her determination to be strong for her husband. "No, it will not be well until Claredon is home. I could not bear to lose him now."

There was a brief silence as Humbly carefully regarded her taut features. Then a faint smile curved his lips. "Because you love him?"

To have her feelings put into words made Victoria momentarily stiffen. She had claimed to love Thomas. It did not seem quite right to compare her feelings for Claredon in the same fashion. After all, what she felt for her husband was nothing at all like what she had felt with Thomas.

With Claredon she was not the mothering caregiver who must solve all problems. Instead, he made her feel respected, cherished, and utterly desirable. They were equals in a way she never could have been with Thomas. And while she had been furious when she had been forced into marriage, it had been more the fact her life had been taken out of her control than true grief that she had lost Thomas. Now the mere thought of losing Claredon left a gaping hole in her heart she knew beyond a doubt would never heal.

"Yes, I love him," she at last admitted in tragic tones. "And I haven't even told him."

Humbly placed a comforting arm about her shoulders. "You will tell him, Victoria. You must have faith."

Salty tears streamed down her cold cheeks. "It is very difficult."

"Well, at least we know he is in the area. He had to have been close by to have noticed the servants hidden in the bushes."

A shudder raced through her at the thought of the villain creeping through the woods, perhaps even stalking around the house itself. And all the while he had poor Claredon bound and perhaps even gagged in some horrid place.

Blast, but she wished she could get her hands upon him. She would make him very, very sorry. She clenched her teeth in frustration. "But we cannot even search for him without putting Claredon at risk."

"It is a difficult situation," Humbly agreed with a sigh.

"It is impossible."

Dropping his arm, Humbly firmly turned her to face him. "He will send another message."

She realized the vicar was only attempting to ease her coiled fear, but her nerves were too brittle to keep her temper in check. She wanted to screech out her rage and hurl the books about the room.

"But then what will we do?" she demanded in sharp tones. "He managed to sense a trap before."

"Yes, it is odd," Humbly grimaced, obviously knowing he had no answer to her logic.

"What is odd?"

Humbly clasped his hands behind his back, his brow furrowed in thought. "We kept the servants well away from the place you were to leave the jewels, and they were hidden in the bushes. We were also very careful to slip them from the house so they would not be noticed."

Victoria gave a shrug, not following his obvious confusion. "He must have been hidden close to the house."

"And risk being caught?" The vicar gave an impatient click of his tongue at the villain's strange behavior. "If he intended to be so close, surely he would have chosen to meet at night? It would have been a simple matter to grab the jewels and slip away before he could be caught."

Victoria herself had been surprised that Mr. Banfield would be so bold as to seek an appointment during the day. As the vicar had pointed out, it would be far safer to expose himself in the dark of night. "What else could it be?" she demanded.

"I do not know." With a sharp movement, Humbly returned to pacing across the room, his head bent as he attempted to sort through the various possibilities. "Unless . . ."

"What?"

He came to a halt, turning to face her. "Maybe he was hiding in the top of one of the trees. I doubt the servants thought to glance upward, and certainly he would have had a clearer view of the house without exposing himself."

Victoria was about to dismiss the absurd notion when her breath abruptly caught in her throat.

The top of the trees.

Of course.

How could she possibly have been so stupid? No wonder the villain had demanded that they meet in that particular location in the woods, and why he had made the appointment during the day.

If he were hidden in Claredon's cottage, he would not only be out of view of others, he would have the telescope to keep a constant watch on the woods. It would be nearly impossible to sneak up to the small clearing without being spotted. And of course, it would be a perfect location to hold Claredon prisoner.

"Victoria, what is it?" Humbly demanded in worried tones.

"The top of the trees," she said in a breathless voice.

"I know, it is absurd . . ."

"No, it is brilliant." She rushed toward him and clasped his hands in a tight grip. "I know where Claredon is."

The vicar regarded her in shock. "You know?"

"It is the only possible place."

"Where is it?"

"I will tell you in a moment, but first we must gather the servants," she said as she was already hurrying from the room. "We must be prepared as soon as it is dark enough to hide us."

Claredon had never been so furious in his entire life.

Gads, he had been a fool to lower his guard just because there had been no sign of Mr. Smith over the past week. It did not help to know he had been mooning over thoughts of his wife when the villain had unexpectedly stepped into pathway with a pistol pointed at his heart.

He was worse than a fool, he told himself. Because of his stupidity, he did not doubt that the crazed man holding a pistol to his head would soon lodge a bullet in him once he had received the treasure he had demanded. He had made no attempt to hide his identity after they had reached the cottage, nor the fact that he was indeed a gentleman of Quality. He could not possibly risk allowing Claredon to live and reveal he had kidnapped and demanded ransom for a nobleman. Even worse, Claredon had put Victoria in danger.

What if the lunatic became angry and decided to punish the innocent woman for preparing a trap to capture him? Or if he realized that Victoria had no jewels to hand over?

Breathing in deeply to fight back a ready sense of panic, Claredon discreetly tested the ropes that bound him to the chair. He already knew they were hopelessly tight, but he had to do something to take his thoughts off the horror of how this night might end.

Careful to keep the pistol pointed at Claredon, the scoundrel folded the note he had just written. Although the man was somewhat younger than Claredon had expected, he bore a remarkable resemblance to the man Victoria had sketched. There was also something faintly familiar about the line of his jaw and the deep set of his eyes, some recognition that tugged just at the edge of Claredon's mind.

"You had better pray your wife shows a bit more sense on this occasion, my lord," he growled, with a desperate edge that sent a chill down Claredon's spine. The man was clearly in dire straits and willing to go to any length to save his worthless skin. "The next time she attempts to be clever she shall discover herself a widow."

Claredon refused to show the fear that pulsed through his blood like a poison. "You'll hang for this, you know."

The man gave a shrill laugh. "Oh no, I have no intention of hanging."

Claredon did not doubt he would do anything to avoid that dreadful fate, including murder. Unfortunately, at the moment he could do nothing more than keep the man talking and hope that rescue eventually came.

"Tell me, Mr. Smith, what jewels are you so desperate to get your hands upon?"

"My dear Aunt Margaret's."

Claredon arched his brows. "You stole from your own aunt?"

The thin lips curled into a sneer at his distasteful tones. "She refused to give me the loan I was in rather desperate need of, so I helped myself to her heirlooms. Unfortunately, her clod-headed son arrived just as I was taking them from the safe, and I was forced to hide them in a figuring that was set on a nearby table. Thomas may be stupid, but even he would notice a bulge of jewels marring the line of my coat."

The gentleman shrugged, unaware of Claredon's suddenly narrowed gaze. "I knew it would be a simple matter to return later and take the figurine. I could not know that the dolt was sending the ugly ornament to his fiancée. It took me weeks to realize that it was no longer in the house."

Claredon sucked in a deep breath, realizing that the man had revealed far more than he intended—not only that the jewels he had stolen had come from Mrs. Stice, but that he was Thomas's cousin. If he could ever get out of here, it would now be a simple matter to track him down.

If he ever got out of here . . . he battled the wave of frustration.

Just keep him talking, Claredon, he told himself. Victoria was incredibly resourceful. If anyone could figure out where they were hidden, she would. He had to hang on to that hope. "And so you came in search of the jewels," he said in remarkably calm tones.

"Oh, yes," he rasped, a dangerous glitter in his pale eyes. "The jewels belong to me. And for my troubles, I have demanded an extra thousand pounds. Perhaps I should make it three thousand."

Claredon frowned at the man's blatant greed. "We do not have three thousand pounds lying about the house."

He smiled with an ugly humor. "Then your sweet wife had best be quick about obtaining a loan. I should hate for her . . ." His taunting words came to an abrupt halt as he whirled toward the closed door. "What was that?"

"What?"

"I heard a noise." Suddenly appearing like a cornered rat, he waved the pistol dangerously in Claredon's direction. "Do not even twitch, my lord, unless you desire a hole through your heart."

Claredon had no intention of moving. Although he had also heard the faint noise, he had faith his servants would not have so clumsily given away their presence unless it was a clever trap. He sincerely hoped that they were deliberately leading the gentleman out of the cottage. He also hoped the man's sudden edge of panic did not force him to presume it was better to do away with his one witness.

Cursing the ropes that kept him firmly bound to the chair, Claredon held his breath as the man cautiously opened the door and peered outside. For a moment nothing occurred, and Claredon nearly cried out in disappointment.

Then, with a sudden flurry of movement, the door was wrenched off its hinges as half a dozen servants tackled the villain and drove him to the ground.

The battle was over before it even began, and Claredon nearly laughed out loud as Johnson delicately stepped over the tangled men in the door to come to his side.

"My lord, are you harmed?" he demanded, the glint in his eyes telling Claredon that he was quite prepared to take any wounds out on his captor's hide.

"No." He glanced over the coachman's shoulder to view the villain being hauled away by the servants. "Is he dead?"

"I do not believe so, my lord. Merely knocked out."

"Good," he said fiercely, shifting so that the servant could cut through the ropes that bound him. "As much as I would love to put a bullet in his gut, I believe I shall take more pleasure in watching him hang."

Bending down to slice the ropes around his ankles Johnson gave a nod of his head. "Yes, sir."

Released from the chair, Claredon rose unsteadily, wincing as the blood rushed back to his hands and feet. For a moment he swayed, nearly falling to his knees. The combination of nerves and hours tied to the chair and made his muscles stiff and his head dizzy. Thankfully, his faithful coachman was swiftly at his side, placing a steadying arm about his waist.

"Thank you, Johnson." He smiled wearily, wanting only to go home and hold his wife in his arms. "Let us return to Longmeade."

* * *

Claredon pulled his wife closer as they snuggled beneath the covers. It had taken far too long to at last find a bit of privacy with Victoria, he thought with a sated sigh.

Returning to Longmeade, he had found the house in chaos. Not only had Victoria called for the local magistrate, but she had also sent for the doctor, who refused to leave until he had thoroughly examined Claredon. By the time the magistrate had been told the full story of Andrew Banfield and hauled him off and the doctor had assured himself all was well, not to mention the large group of servants who wished to see for themselves the desperado had not harmed their master, the night was nearly spent.

That had not halted him, however, from seeking the comfort of Victoria's embrace the moment the house had settled to sleep.

Their coming together had been tinged with a bittersweet urgency at the realization of how close they had come to losing one another. Claredon had held her tightly in his arms, his entire body filled with a shimmering happiness at the knowledge they now had their whole lives together.

Running her hands over the arm that was laid over her stomach, Victoria winced as she felt the scrapes upon his wrist from the ropes that had bound him.

"My poor Claredon," she murmured.

"Poor, indeed," he agreed, softly stroking the tender skin of her temple with his lips. He inhaled deeply of her scent, wondering what he had ever done to be fortunate enough to have this woman in his life. "I shall be in need of endless care to fully recover."

He had meant to tease a smile from her, but Victoria swiftly stiffened in lingering anger and fury at Andrew Banfield. "To think that lout would . . ."

"No." He placed a finger upon her lips, far too comfortable to recall the horrid events of the day. "We have seen the last of Banfield. No good can come of dwelling upon the past—although I must say I am very impressed with how you managed to discover my whereabouts."

She snuggled even closer, stirring all sorts of interesting sensations. "Yes, I thought I was rather clever myself."

He gave a low chuckle. "Modesty as well as beauty. An irresistible combination."

"I should have realized the truth much sooner," she admitted with a hint of annoyance. "It was not until Vicar Humbly mentioned his confusion over how Mr. Banfield managed to spot the hidden servants, as well as his odd decision to meet during the day, that I realized he must have used the telescope in the cottage to keep track of our movements."

Allowing his fingers to stroke the perfect satin of her cheek, he heaved a rueful sigh. "It was a foolish mistake to leave the ladder down so the villain could discover the cottage."

She abruptly turned to face him, her expression fierce in the dim candlelight. "No, I am glad that you did. He was determined to kidnap you, and had he taken you somewhere else we might never have found you."

He smiled gently. "Well, as the famous old bard once said, 'all's well that ends well.'"

"Yes."

"I presume that Mr. Stice will soon be leaving?" he demanded, careful to keep his voice bland. Although he no longer believed Thomas Stice was in any way involved with his cousin, he could not wholly deny a burning desire to be rid of his presence. He had no wish to share Victoria with anyone, including annoying ex-fiancés.

"Indeed." She gave a dry chuckle. "He took to his bed soon after we discovered his mother's jewels and would not leave until he was certain his cousin had been hauled away in chains. Now he is anxious to return to London to prove to his mother he had nothing to do with the theft."

"Good riddance," he muttered.

"Claredon."

He refused to apologize for his seething dislike. "For such a buffoon, the man caused us no end of trouble, first by stealing your sympathy and then by giving you a figurine filled with stolen loot."

"In all fairness, he did not know about the jewels," she said softly.

"How about the months of jealousy I endured while you believed yourself to be in love with him?"

"You, jealous?" She arched her brows in a teasing fashion. "I do not believe it."

He gave a low growl as he pulled her even closer. "Horridly, wretchedly jealous."

She pretended to give the matter some thought as she lightly ran her fingers over his arm. Claredon shuddered with a slowly simmering desire. Gads, this woman had only to be near for him to be consumed with need. A most unnerving sensation.

"Well, he is responsible in some vague fashion for the two of us being together."

Claredon grimaced, refusing to concede anything to the bumbling fool. "I far prefer to believe that it was fate. I cannot imagine any other woman but you as my wife."

Her eyes darkened at his words, a suddenly

somber expression descending upon her pale features. "Claredon?"

"Yes, my minx?"

There was a long pause before she at last cleared her throat in a nervous fashion. "There is something I desire to say to you."

Claredon felt his heart stop. They had come through so much to at last be together. Surely to goodness she was not having regrets? He did not believe he could bear the blow.

"That sounds rather dire," he attempted to tease, too frightened to breathe.

"No, not dire, only . . ."

Clamping onto his nerves, Claredon reached out to gently cup her cheek. Whatever she had to tell him, he never wished her to fear to speak the truth. It was past time for honesty in their relationship. "Victoria, you can tell me anything," he whispered.

Ominously her gaze dropped before she at last managed to speak. "I . . . I love you."

Sharp, disbelieving relief rushed through him, making him feel as giddy as if he had consumed a dozen bottles of champagne. Unable to halt himself, he tilted back his head to laugh with bone-deep joy.

Clearly offended by his unusual reaction to her confession of love, Victoria glared at him in embarrassed anger. "What is so funny?"

Attempting to restrain his mirth, Claredon swooped downward to seal her lips with a kiss of pure possession. "You sounded more as if you were confessing that you burned down the barn or overturned the carriage rather than your undying devotion."

Not at all appeased by his teasing words, she sent

him a speaking glare. "I wish I had not said anything now."

With a swift movement he rolled atop her, trap-
ping her face in his hands. He briefly wondered if a
gentleman's heart could actually burst from sheer
happiness. "Oh, no, you cannot take it back now," he
informed her in firm tones, his gaze memorizing
every fascinating detail of her face. "No matter how
you say you love me, it fills my heart with joy."

"And a great deal of amusement, obviously." She
sulked.

Placing a delicate kiss upon her brow, he leaned
back to regard her with an unwavering gaze. "Forgive
me, my dearest," he murmured. "I know it was not a
simple matter to be the one to first say the words, so
I will make it easier by admitting that I love you." He
kissed the tip of her nose. "I adore you." He kissed
her stubborn chin. "I cherish you." He brushed the
fullness of her lips. "You are truly the woman of my
fantasies come to life."

Her expression melted as she placed her arms
about his neck, her eyes shimmering as brightly as
emeralds in the shadowed light. "Claredon."

"Oh my sweet, God truly was watching over us to
ensure two such stubborn, thick-skulled fools managed to find one another."

She gave a faint shiver. "It was a near thing, was it
not?"

Claredon could not even allow himself to contemplate the odd tangle of circumstances that had
brought this woman to him. How easily it might have
been never to have realized that Victoria was the only
true woman for him, and how easily she might have
ended up tied for a lifetime to Thomas Stice.

His stomach clenched as he gave a slow shake of

his head. "Too near," he growled in rough tones. "To even consider the possibility that we might not be together is unbearable."

She smiled wryly at his fierce tone. "All because you slipped into my room with the intent of seduction."

Seduction.

A wicked expression replaced his frown. Now that was a subject far more interesting at the moment.

"Just the beginning of a lifetime of nights I intend to slip into your room with the intent of seduction," he promised, his hands moving in a determined path over her delicate curves.

She lifted her brows in mock surprise. "My lord, whatever are you about?"

His pulse raced as the ever ready desire coursed through his blood. "Well, I did manage to purchase the land before I was so rudely kidnapped. We shall have need of heirs to appreciate our efforts."

Her lips twitched at his logic. "Very conscientious of you."

"Well, family duty is family duty," he sighed.

"Of course."

His hands became more determined as he sought to stir the embers of her own desire. "And besides, if I am to return to my bed, I must have some comfort to keep me until we can be together again."

Without warning, her hands moved to frame his face. "No."

Rather taken aback by her unexpected rejection, Claredon gave a startled blink. "No?"

"I want you to stay."

"Here?" he demanded in disbelief.

"Yes."

It was, he knew, the last barrier she possessed, and he tumbled into love with her all over again. It went beyond modesty to the very essence of her heart. She had at last committed herself utterly to him, with no lingering doubts as to her feelings.

"Are you certain?" he demanded, not wishing to push her beyond what she desired to give freely.

She smiled deep into his searching gaze. "I do not intend to be parted from you ever again."

"You will get no argument from me, my dearest," he whispered as his head lowered. "No argument at all."

Fifteen

Vicar Humbly was forced to call upon every scrap of his Christian charity, not to mention having to bite his tongue more than once.

It was not that the new vicar was in any way a bad man. Indeed, Humbly was quite certain that he was determined to do his very best for the people in the neighborhood.

But while he attempted to reassure himself that the church would be in competent hands, Humbly could not deny a certain sadness as he glanced about the shabby vicarage that had been thoroughly cleaned and refurbished with a stiff formality that said much of the young, rigidly reserved man.

How would he react when the local tenants came tramping through his tidy home with their muddy boots and faithful hounds at their side? Or when the children came racing and tumbling in to search for the bits of candy he always kept ready in the parlor?

He gave an inward sigh.

Thoroughly unaware of Humbly's dark thoughts, Mr. Roster glanced primly about the library with obvious satisfaction at the barren cleanliness. "As you can see, I have created an entirely new filing system." He waved a hand toward the desk. "It is far tidier than tossing important documents about in a haphazard manner."

Humbly cleared his throat, well aware that he was being gently chastised for his lack of organization. "Oh, yes," he murmured. "Yes, indeed."

"And I reorganized the books." The thin, rather sharp-featured man shot Humbly a pointed glance. "Really, I do not know how you managed to find the necessary references."

Humbly shrugged, not about to admit that he rarely bothered with references when writing his sermons. To his mind speaking from the heart and in a language that could be understood by all was far more important. "I suppose I muddled through."

Mr. Roster heaved a long-suffering sigh. "I have yet to begin on the church records. I fear they will demand a considerable amount of effort."

"It appears that you have been very busy."

"It is my duty."

Resisting the urge to point out attending to the needs of the parishioners was surely his first duty, Humbly gently cleared his throat. "I do hope you have had the opportunity to acquaint yourself with your neighbors?"

"Certainly. Any number have come to the vicarage for a visit." His features tightened with a vague disapproval. "Indeed, I have been astonished to discover that you were in the habit of encouraging your congregation to call whenever they pleased."

"To be honest, I enjoyed visiting with them," Humbly confessed.

A thin smile curved the thin lips. "Very proper, of course, but hardly the best use of your time. There must be routine established if God's work is to be done. I have requested that all visits be confined to the hours between two and five. Far more tidy than having people interrupting me all hours of the day."

"Very tidy," Humbly forced himself to agree, deeply relieved that Mrs. Stalwart had elected to join him at his tiny cottage. He would not wish to hear what she would have to say about the new vicar's rigid schedule.

"Would you care to see what I have done with the study?"

Humbly managed to conceal a shudder. His Christian charity was, unfortunately, not boundless.

"Not today, thank you," he said hastily. "Mrs. Stalwart will be expecting me home soon."

"How disappointing." There was a perfunctory edge to his voice. "I do hope you will call again."

Humbly simply could not resist. God, he was quite certain, had a lovely sense of humor. "Yes, between the hours of two and five on the next occasion."

Blithely unaware that he had just been insulted, Mr. Roster gave a nod of his head. "Perhaps that would be for the best."

"No doubt. Now I bid you good day." With a polite bow, Humbly gathered his hat and set off on the long walk to his cottage.

"Humbly, you are an old fool." He chastised himself for his petty dislike, knowing that at least a portion of it came from his own reluctance to acknowledge he was no longer vicar. He would no doubt find fault with anyone, especially a man so vastly different from himself. "Time to make room for the younger generation."

Still . . . there was no denying that the man was a bit of a twit, a renegade voice whispered in the back of his mind.

Shaking his head at the follies of both Mr. Roster and himself, Humbly trudged down the path.

Perhaps the problem was that he had not yet fully accepted his decision to retire to his tiny cottage, he at last acknowledged. It was not that he did not find the small home just as cozy and peaceful as he had desired, nor that he did not enjoy puttering about in his gardens. It was more a realization he was no longer needed.

He heaved a faint sigh.

There was something very satisfying at the thought he could bring comfort to a sick widow or lend a quiet word of encouragement to a disheartened tenant or even allow the local squire to vent his spleen upon his own head rather than the heads of his poor servants.

Perhaps his small skills would never change the world, but they did make a difference in the lives he cared for. He would miss that feeling of being depended upon.

Feeling oddly blue deviled, Humbly finished the walk to his cottage and entered the tiny foyer without his usual bounce. He removed his hat, not surprised when Mrs. Stalwart hurried to join him.

Since leaving the vicarage, the older housekeeper had been even more inclined to cluck over him like a mother hen. "Well, Mr. Humbly, it is about time you returned."

His smile returned at her chiding tone. It would not be home without her ceaseless scoldings. "Forgive me, but I decided to stop by the vicarage for a visit."

Her round countenance tightened with obvious disapproval. "Well then, it is no wonder you look as cross as crabs. That man is enough to put anyone out of sorts."

Feeling a pang of guilt that he secretly agreed with the housekeeper's assessment, Humbly gave a shake of his head. "Now, Mrs. Stalwart, he appears to be quite . . . organized."

"A pompous fool," she retorted with a snort.

Weary of brooding upon Mr. Roster, Humbly sought to distract the tenacious woman, who no doubt could go on several hours. "I believe I might have a small sherry before luncheon," he murmured.

With astonishing speed, Mrs. Stalwart lost her dark frown and instead offered him a rather sly smile. "I beg your pardon, Vicar, but you have a guest awaiting you in the garden."

Humbly lifted his brow in surprise. It was all too rare that he had company now that he had left the vicarage. "A guest? Who is it?"

Her smile only became more sly. "I believe that you should see for yourself."

Humbly cast his housekeeper a startled gaze. It was entirely unlike Mrs. Stalwart to be coy. Indeed, she was without a doubt the most bluntly spoken woman he had ever encountered. "Goodness, you are being rather mysterious."

"Why do you not go along? I shall bring a nice tray of tea."

Wondering who on earth could have caused that distinct twinkle in the older woman's eyes, Humbly gave a slow nod of his head. "Very well."

More than a little intrigued, Humbly made his way toward the back of the house. He did hope whoever it was intended to remain for a few hours. It would be good to have a nice chat with an old acquaintance. Perhaps he could even convince them to stay for dinner and a game of chess over a nice glass of port.

Reaching the narrow door that led to the garden, Humbly pushed it open and stepped into the warm sunlight. For a moment he was too blinded by the sudden light to notice more than a number of large shadows about the garden. Then, as his eyes slowly adjusted, his jaw dropped in shock.

"Oh," he muttered. "Oh."

The three couples quietly talking beside his prize rosebushes abruptly turned at his incoherent exclamation.

Addy was there with her husband Adam, Beatrice with her devoted Gabriel, and, of course, Victoria with Claredon.

As if on cue, the three women linked arms and moved forward to greet him with wide smiles. Not quite able to believe his eyes, Humbly regarded the vibrant, lovely women he had come to love as his own daughters—Addy with her irrepressible spirit, Beatrice with her quiet intelligence, and Victoria with her glorious beauty. All three so different, and yet so much alike with their kind hearts and generous natures.

"Mr. Humbly," Addy greeted as they came to a halt directly in front of his shocked form.

"Addy, what on earth is going on?"

She gave him a saucy grin. "We wished to welcome you to your new home."

"And to thank you for all you have done for us," Beatrice added, a deep sense of contentment about her that greatly relieved Humbly's spirit.

"But . . ." Flustered by this unexpected treat, he found himself blushing like the veriest schoolboy. "You need not have traveled all this way to see me."

Addy gave a click of her tongue. "We would have traveled to the colonies, if necessary. Besides, we wished to see your lovely cottage."

For once in his sixty years, Humbly found himself without words. Just the knowledge that these dear women would come all this way to visit him made his heart glow with pleasure. "Oh, well, it is not much," he warned.

"Nonsense. It is just as comfortable as you said it was."

Turning toward the titian-haired maiden, he offered a small smile. "Victoria, my dearest. How are you?"

"Very well," she replied, with a glow that was almost tangible.

"Really, you should not have gone to such trouble to come all this way," he chastised, well aware that she and Claredon were no doubt anxious for some time alone.

She reached out to pat his arm. "I assure you that it was no trouble. We wished to be here with you."

"Do you suppose we could have a tour of your new home?" Beatrice demanded.

"Certainly, though there is little to tour," he warned.

Addy gave him a mysterious smile. "Oh, you might be surprised."

Not certain what she meant by the odd words, Humbly turned to lead them back into the house, rather surprised when the three maidens followed him on their own. Coming to a halt, he regarded the gentlemen still standing in the garden with a raised brow. "Surely you do not intend to leave your husbands behind?"

"I believe they will be able to entertain themselves," Beatrice assured him.

Victoria gave a soft chuckle. "Indeed, they appear to be enjoying each other's company."

"No doubt they are busily discussing the wondrous qualities of their wives," Addy said with a smile.

"Or perhaps they are debating who is the most stubborn," Beatrice suggested.

"Indeed." Addy gave a shrug, then linked her arm with Humbly's. "We will leave them to their fun. Come along, Mr. Humbly."

With a firm purpose, Addy led Humbly back through the cottage, surprisingly steering him straight toward the tiny library set off the parlor. Opening the door, she stepped aside and waited for him to enter first.

Sensing that the three maidens were up to something, Humbly cautiously entered the room and came to a startled stop.

Wide-eyed, he glanced about the bookshelves that had been suddenly filled with leather-bound books. Just that morning, they had appeared nearly barren beyond the few volumes he had taken from the vicarage. It was like a miracle.

"Oh, my."

Victoria chuckled as she stepped up beside him. "We each chose our favorite books to buy. I chose a number of the classics and philosophers, Beatrice found a large number of travel journals, and Addy bought every gothic novel and book of poetry she could lay her hands upon."

"My dears." His voice broke as he battled tears of joy. "This is too much."

"It is just a small way of telling you thank you for all that you have done. Not only for us, but the neighborhood as well," Addy told him in firm tones.

"And to ensure you are never bored in your retirement," Beatrice added.

Just the fact that they would go to such an effort made Humbly feel as if he were the most fortunate gentleman in all of England. "I do not know what to say," he at last muttered.

"There is nothing to be said," Beatrice informed him with a tender smile. "Just be happy."

"Nothing could make me happier than having you three here."

Addy gave a sudden laugh. "Well, I do hope you mean that, since we intend to visit quite regularly."

"Yes, indeed," Beatrice chimed in. "We have no intention of neglecting our own private Cupid."

Humbly smiled widely, suddenly far more pleased with his tiny cottage and simple life. "You will always be welcome here."

"Well, just to make sure, we have one more surprise," Victoria told him, moving across the room to pull a large basket from behind the desk. "We have all discovered the way to your heart."

Clasping his hands together, Humbly breathed in the scent that suddenly filled the air, his eyes closing with delight. "Lemon tarts . . ."

ABOUT THE AUTHOR

DEBBIE RALEIGH lives with her family in Missouri. She is currently working on her next Zebra regency romance, *My Lord Vampire,* which will be published in August 2003. Debbie loves to hear from readers, and you may write to her c/o Zebra Books. Please include a self-addressed stamped envelope if you wish a response.

Discover the Romances of

Hannah Howell

The Queen of
Romance

Cassie Edwards

DO YOU HAVE THE
HOHL COLLECTION?